Sissy Dollhouse

Season Two

2018 Jenna Masters

Contents

Sissy Bimbo Drone Lost and Found

He wore black fatigues and drove a jeep like he was military but he was a private security guard. He drove along a run of fence, in the dark of night. The nights on the island were darker than he was used to back in Los Angeles, but the pay, at this strange island resort, was unbeatable.

John pulled the jeep to the side of the rough dirt road and took his automatic rifle from the gun rack. He pointed it a pale figure down in the field and activated the magnification on his scope. He smiled, shook his head and put his rifle back in the rack. He picked up the radio and told the dispatch officer, "I'm at sector Charlie Niner. It's not an intruder. One of Tanya's dolls got loose again."

The voice of dispatched crackled over the radio. "Make sure you get it before it hurts itself. Those dolls pay your salary, and you don't want to see how upset Ms. Pain gets when one of her Toys gets damaged."

"Yes sir," John said, smiling to himself when he thought about the slender, six foot tall blonde who ruled the island like her own private empire. The woman would be his biggest fantasy, except for the fact that he was terrified to even think of her inappropriately, as if she could see into his thoughts and would devour him in a single bite if he thought something she didn't approve of. "I'll make sure the doll is delivered back home smiling and pretty."

"I'll mark you as off your rounds for the next hour," dispatch said. "But don't play too long."

It was an unspoken rule that finding a lost sissy-doll entitled a guard to a special kind of bonus. John hung up his radio and started walking down to the field where the little blonde figure wandered aimlessly. As he got closer he could see that the slim figure was naked. She had blank, distant blue eyes and soft hair that fell in waves over her slender shoulders. She was pale and impossibly thin with gorgeous, full, C-cup tits. She had full lips and flawless skin and tight, feminine curves. There was nothing to give away the fact that she had been born a man, except for the thin, hairless penis that hung from her smooth crotch. She had long, slim legs.

As John got closer she looked at him with wide, curious eyes.

"Hey Sweetheart," John said.

"I think I'm lost," she said. She had a lovely smile as she looked at him with an airheaded expression on her pretty face.

"That's alright," John said. "What's your name?"

"Jen," the sissy answered, smiling as if very proud of herself for knowing the answer to his question.

"Come on, Jen," he said. "I'll take you home."

"Home?" she asked. She looked around the dark field. "I think I'd rather stay here."

The sissy toys that lived here and served as the entertainment for the rich clientele who visited the island were always docile and eager to follow instructions, so John could just tell her what to do and she would obey, but John hesitated. He wasn't used to standing up to women. He had always been shy around women, especially beautiful ones. Even his wife made him nervous and kept him on edge, and she wasn't half as beautiful as this little doll. Somehow though, the limp little penis hanging between the sissy's slender thighs made it easier to take charge of the doll. He simply told her, "It's time to come with me."

He turned to walk and felt a rush when she actually obeyed, following docilely behind him.

"Am I in trouble?" she asked.

"I don't have any idea what goes on inside the compound," he said. "That's a whole different set of guards. But I don't think you're in trouble." As they got back to the road the stopped in front of the jeep. He turned the lights on so he could get a better look at the sexy little doll. It was amazing really. John was not someone who would have ever considered being with a tranny of any kind, he was as straight as an arrow. He had a very pretty young wife at home in the United States, and every six weeks when he cycled home for leave he enjoyed every minute of his time with her. But he had never been with a woman as gorgeous and glamourous looking as these little sissies Tanya Pain created.

Jen stood in the glow from the headlights of the Jeep, completely unashamed of her slender, hairless body as she stared into John's eyes. She had a serene, thoughtless look on her blank face. She had that intense, artificial sex-appeal of a Hollywood starlet. Nothing about the little blonde was original, nothing about her was natural. She was Tanya Pain's complete creation, and she was completely flawless.

John walked around her, looking her up and down, from her full round ass to her long blonde hair; from her bimbo looking face to her pretty, painted toes. "When was the last time you had a cock in your mouth?" John asked her. He was surprised he could build up the nerve to speak to her like that, but her true, sissy nature made it easier to treat her like the little slut she was.

She licked her lips, tongue wet with saliva, as if the mere suggestion of a cock in her mouth had activated some switch in her broken, little mind. "I don't remember," she said.

"What about that tight little ass of yours? When was the last time it was fucked nice and hard?"

Jen moaned. Her little dick was swelling as her gorgeous tits rose higher from her deepening breathing. "I don't remember," she practically moaned. "A long time I think."

John continued circling the slender doll. He ran his fingertips along her flawless skin as if confirming she wasn't some kind of mirage. Finally, he stopped in front of her. "Beg me to let you suck it," he said. "Beg me to let you suck my cock." He felt mad with power. He had never in his life spoken to a woman like that.

Her small hands moved forward, touching the fabric of his fatigue pants, her palms running softly down his thigh. "Please," she purred with authentic sounding need. "Please. I want to suck it. I need to suck it. Please let me suck your big, gorgeous cock."

Her words came out with intense, purring feeling, but her face was still blank, staring at him with eyes that could belong to a curious animal. "Fuck your hot," John said.

"Cock," Jen purred, her voice desperate like a junky. "Please. I need to suck your cock right now or I think I'll die. Cock. Please give me your cock."

John undid his belt and let his pants fall to his combat boots. His massive hard-on stood proud and throbbing, pointing up at the sissy doll's full, Botox enhanced lips. Jen had her own erection, but she seemed much more interested in John's. She dropped to her small knees on the dirt road and reached up to him with both hands. One small hand cupped his fat, hairy balls while the other stroked his pulsating cock. Her fingertips caressed his balls with soft, careful brushing, barely making contact. Her other hand was wrapped tightly around his shaft, squeezing his tight meat in her soft grasp.

She looked up at him, her head turned slightly sideways like a dog listening for something. "Can I?" she asked again. "Can I suck it, please?"

"Yes," John said. "You can suck it, you filthy little sex doll."

"Thank you," Jen purred as she turned her blue eyes from his face down to his throbbing cock and spread her bright red lips wide.

John moaned as she slipped his fat cock into her little, wet, sissy mouth. She made noises like his dick was the most delicious piece of meat that had ever touched her tongue as she drove her wet lips down his shaft. Her mouth was stretched wide around his fat cock, her jaw looking unhinged, but she had no problem driving him down her narrow throat. John looked down at her full, round ass and tiny waist as she knelt on the dirt and deep-throated him.

Her own small erection was throbbing between her smooth, slender thighs as sucked and stroked him eagerly. She began to bounce her head back and forth along the length of his big rod. Drool dripped off his cock and balls in the cold night air as she slurped up and down his hard-on. John sighed, the sensation of the sissy's mouth and throat and eager tongue all felt amazing on his hot prick. He had never had a woman suck him this good and he wondered what Tanya did to train her dolls to be such fantastic cock-suckers.

"That's a good whore," John told her. "That's a good little bimbo sex slave."

The little sissy doll's face glowed with pride as he praised her. She sucked him faster, blonde hair bouncing with the movement of her small, pretty head. Her hands ran up and down his thighs, gently caressing his skin with her fingertips. Her tongue stroked the underside of his penis and she hummed gently on his cock. The suction of her mouth and throat was powerful and intense and John felt harder than he'd ever been in his life. He touched her with his hands as if to remind himself she was real. He felt the silkiness of her hair and the softness of her skin as his hands brushed her pretty face.

"I bet you live to suck cock, don't you Slut?" John said. "I bet Tanya puts it into your dreams every night, whispering it into your ear."

She didn't hesitate or slow her pace, but kept driving her talented little mouth back and forth along the throbbing length of his hard cock. Her full lips squeezed against his hot flesh, her mouth working like she was starving for dick.

John moaned as the soft lips of her skilled little mouth squeezed the throbbing meat of his big cock. Her head bobbed as she knelt naked in the dirt, sucking him off in the cold night air. A thin line of drool ran down his shaft to his balls, and then dripped like a glistening dew drop, down from his sack to the ground. She made a messy, guttural noise as she hungrily slurped him. She seemed as if her greatest and most treasured dream was to suck every ounce of juice out of his balls through the straw if his cock. Her cheeks were pulled in, her lips pursed out, her tongue pressed against him, her silky blonde hair bouncing, her gorgeous tits jiggling as her whole torso moved back and back and forth.

John was seconds away from blowing his load in her soft little mouth but stopped himself. He wanted to feel that tranny's tight, feminine ass. He put his hand on her forehead to stop her back and forth movement. She looked up at him, desperate need burning in her eyes as then slipped his glistening cock from between her pillowy lips.

"Please," she begged once more. "Please. I need to suck it. I need to suck more cock."

He took her by the hair and guided her to her feet, then pushed her up against the hood of the security patrol jeep.

He held her by the hair as he whispered into her ear; "I'm going to shove it in your ass first." He bent her over the hood, pressing her naked torso down against the steel, still warm from engine heat. He pushed her tight against the front of the jeep, her small, sissy-hard-on smashed against the grill as he spread her soft round ass-cheeks with the fingers of one hand and took his throbbing, spit covered erection in the other. He leaned down and spit onto the crack of her smooth, feminine ass, letting his spittle run down to her asshole before he pushed the head of his fat cock to her tight opening. \

He reached up and took a handful of her beautiful blonde hair. He wrapped his hand in her hair like a rodeo cowboy wrapping his hand around the lead of a wild horse, than he plunged his fat cock deep inside her.

She whimpered in a high, broken voice as his dick pushed into the depths of her tight, sissy-cunt. Her soft warmth engulfed him as he pushed deep inside her asshole. She moaned with deep, primal surrender as she yielded to his hard prick. John grunted, burying himself to the base in the dollified sissy's gorgeous little ass. Her ass-cheeks felt silky soft as they smashed against his hips, and his weight pressed her hard against the grill.

Jen's small hard on pressed against the grill of the jeep, her face and tits resting on the hood, sliding back and forth along the steel as John's hands pulled her towards him and his cock pummeled her away. Every thrust of his big cock was echoed in her voice which was shrill and feminine and full of both pleasure and pain. Her pretty, vacant eyes showed a hint of her true consciousness beneath the haze, a deep awareness that she was being used as a fuckdoll by a more powerful man.

"Yes," Jen's voice whispered. "Yes."

"Such a pretty little bitch," John moaned. "Such a soft, pretty little bitch."

The sweet little tranny's ass was tight and felt silky smooth as John drove his throbbing meat deep into her slender body. His hand in her hair and his hand on her curved hip rocked her back against him as every thrust sent her smashing back down into the front of the jeep. She was whimpering with pleasure, driving her little ass back against him with eager need as he smashed down on her.

John could feel the sissy getting more and more excited, her body moving with more animation. Her slender back arched and she leaned up, reaching behind herself to grab the back of John's neck. She seemed as if she wanted every part of her gorgeous little body to be in contact with him. He reached across the front of her and cupped one of her fantastic tits as he continued to rock his hard body against her soft, tight little frame. He was grinding her against the front of the jeep as he plunged himself inside her, her erection rubbing against the metal as she whimpered. He could feel the small muscles of her tight, slender torso tightening as her whimpering quickened to a steady wail. She rode against him, her eyes closed, her hands in fists, her mouth open wide. He could feel the sheath of her soft ass locking down on him, pulling tight against the ridges of his gently curving cock as a powerful orgasm rocked through her slim body.

"Yes," she whimpered. "Yes."

He fought through her tightened ass to give her a few more solid thrusts, holding her firmly by the tits and the hip. His cock was still hard and ready as he began to slide it out of her little, bleached asshole. As he pulled her away from the jeep, John saw that the sissy's orgasm had caused her to spill cum all over the grill of the patrol vehicle.

"Look at the mess you made," he told her. She stared down at her own semen glistening in the cold night air. He pushed her down to her knees and ordered her to, "Be a good girl and clean that up."

She instantly went to work, licking the cum splattered grill of his jeep. He watched, one hand still wrapped in her gorgeous blonde hair, the other stroking his own, raging hard-on as the little bimbo sissy licked in long, eager strokes, her vacant eyes looking up at him for approval. She licked both dirt and her own semen as her tongue bathed the front of the dirty, patrol vehicle. Her tiny body, highlighted with soft dramatic curves, was the most beautiful thing he'd ever seen and her eager mouth, working around the metal ridges on the front of his jeep to eat cum was one of the nastiest.

The sight of it was too much for John. He couldn't hold back anymore. His cock twitched in his hand as his balls tightened. He groaned as he stared down at the beautiful, blank-faced Barbie-doll, and he began to shoot his semen. She smiled as the first steamy wad of sperm splattered her in the center of the forehead and began to drip down the bridge of her dainty nose. She continued cleaning the grill, looking at him as he shot cum in her face. He sprayed heaping wads of hot sperm onto the sissy's sexy face and beautiful hair, drenching her in cum as she continued to lick on the grill, seeming happy to take that filthy shower he was pouring onto her.

When he finished cumming he caught his breath and seeing her still at work licking the front of his jeep he said, "Okay. Okay Sweetheart. That's good. That's good enough.

She turned and smiled up at him, half of her face and hair dripping with his seed. "All clean?" she asked.

"All clean," he told her.

John pulled up his fatigues and got a dirty rag from the jeep. He handed it to the filthy tranny. "We better clean off your face before I take you back to Ms. Pain." She used the oily rag to wipe up the semen as best as she could. John took her by the thin, weak arm, guiding her into the back of the Jeep. He got behind the wheel and started to drive towards the entrance to the inner compound. He thought once again about the breathtaking blonde who ran the place. He was feeling a combination of excitement and dread that he might see Tanya Pain when he got there. He had seen her many times but never actually talked to the woman, and suddenly, he couldn't decide if that was a good thing or not. He drove on with a strange, ominous feeling.

Bending his Shy Little Mind

John stood in a room near the entry to the underground bunker where the dolls were kept. He had just returned Jen to guard that manned the entrance, but had been told to wait for Ms. Pain. He waited with a combination of excitement and terror. Everyone here was afraid of the beautiful but cruel and intensely powerful Tanya Pain, but him even more than others. He had always been intimidated by powerful women as well as beautiful women, and Tanya was both those things in once.

She strolled into the room. She was as gorgeous as he remembered. She was slender and curvaceous with long, blonde hair and powerful blue eyes. She had an unwavering stare and a perfect posture and stride. She wore a black skirt suit, her white blouse open to expose the beginning of her fantastic cleavage. Her long, nylon-covered legs were utterly flawless. She wore long, spiked heeled shoes. Without them, she would stand eye to eye with John, who was a fraction over six feet tall.

Tanya looked him up and down with her ice blue eyes. Her powerful presence was unsettling. John swallowed and smiled. "I found her in the outer zones," he said, even though hadn't asked him anything.

Tanya didn't seem to be listening. She continued to appraise him. "My my… aren't you delicious," she said.

John didn't know what to say, so he said nothing.

The silence seemed overwhelming and just when John was about to break it Tanya spoke once more. "Did you fuck her?" she asked.

John's heart froze. All the guards said it was allowed, even expected that you fuck the dolls before you return them. He had suspected that if he didn't fuck this one, everyone would make fun of him when he got back to the barracks. But what if he had it backwards? He knew a night with one of these dolls cost more than he made in several of his six week rotations to the island. What if he just got himself into terrible trouble?

"It's a simple question," Tanya said. "Did you fuck my sissy doll in her tight little ass before you brought her back to me?"

John was terrified. He couldn't find his voice.

Tanya laughed suddenly. "You're kind of a pussy for a security guard, aren't you?"

John wasn't afraid of combat. He'd served in the army and he had been shot at, but no matter how much he did, he was still terrified of a really powerful, beautiful woman. At twenty five years old he still had no idea how to talk to women like that. And of all the beautiful and powerful women he'd cowered in front of over the years, none of them were as powerful or as beautiful as Tanya Pain.

He knew he had to stand up for himself but his head was spinning. He was relieved when Tanya suddenly laughed and said, "I'm just teasing you. You are simply adorable. How tall are you?"

"Six feet," he said.

She was circling him, "And yet so slender," she said.

She stopped in front of him and said. "How would you like to come entertain me in my room, if you're not too tired from fucking my doll?"

"Yes, I mean. Yes. I'd like to come to your room. Whatever you want, Ms. Pain."

"Good boy," Tanya purred beginning to lead him away. "What's your dress size?"

"What?" John asked.

"Never mind," Tanya teased. "We'll figure it out. I'm going to have a lot of fun with you."

Tanya felt the young guard's eyes glued to her ass as he walked nervously behind her. She led him to one of her rooms. She had fallen behind in her doll recruitment in the last few months, so she was happy to know that she had a suitable trainee already working for her. He was perhaps a little more macho than most of the boys she brought back to the compound, but that was all just window dressing. Guns and soldering and sex: Affectation just there to hide the weak, little sissy soul quivering inside him. Tanya could spot it from a mile away. She knew from experience that this needy little soldier would break easy, and break completely. His thin veil of forced masculinity would wipe away like grime on a delicate crystal statue.

She led him into the room. He was tall and skinny. He looked like a runner but he had fine, soft features, dark hair and compelling green eyes. She walked across the room, giving him another chance to stare at her when he didn't think she was watching. She turned on some hypnotic music: a pulsing rhythm of waves proven to affect the male brain, causing deep relaxation, openness and suggestibility. She poured him a drug laced drink and pressed it into his slender, long fingered hands.

"How do you feel?" she asked.

"Kind of strange," he admitted.

She smiled and began to circle him. Her heels clicked in the floor like a metronome. "If you're nervous I want you to know you don't have to be. This place is a special place." The strange droning music was already affecting him, as were the psychotropic drugs in his drink. "This is a special place because there is no judgement. There is only deep, wonderful relaxation. Everything that usually makes you nervous, here, makes you even more relaxed. Everything that usually fills you with fear… here it fills you with warmth and excitement." Her hypnotic voice droned as he stood, swaying slightly. "In this room, your worst nightmares could become true, and it would be the most wonderful feeling in the world."

She stopped in front of him. "You can believe me. I will never, ever lie to you." She stood close, giving him a chance to look down her blouse but he was careful not to.

"You are really, very shy, aren't you?" Tanya said in her hypnotic voice; soft and drifting with an irresistible sultry lilt.

"I know I shouldn't be I..."

"You're wrong," she interrupted him. "You should be shy. You're right to be shy. You should wander around in a constant state of deep, delicious shame." She moved around him again touching him freely with her agile, teasing hands. "Your shyness is your deeper mind telling you that you are not worthy, that you're less than other people. Especially less than other people like me; but that goes without saying. You hide it well. But deep in your trembling little soul, you are a weak and worthless little thing."

She could see that John wanted to argue but the drugs and his own natural insecurities were making it difficult. Deep down he already knew that what she was saying was what everyone else secretly thought but was too polite to say. The music and the drugs were already scrambling his brain, making him even more susceptible than his naturally weak mind already was.

Tanya pushed the drink in his hand up to his lips. "Finish your drink," she gently commanded. "Make sure and swallow every drop."

John lifted the drink to his lips and continued to down it as she circled him, still purring in her compelling voice. "Think of it as medicine. I'm going to cure you tonight. I'm going to cure you of a very troublesome delusion that society has inflicted upon you."

John felt so relaxed he could barely stand. His legs swayed and his head felt light and empty.

Tanya put her hands on him and guided him down to seating. "Do you want that? Do you want me to cure you? Do you want to finally be free of the delusion and the lie that you're just as good as other people?"

John hesitated to answer.

"Say yes," Tanya purred into his ear.

"Yes," John moaned.

"Good boy," Tanya purred rewardingly.

She clicked her heels on the floor as she began to circle him once more, counting down from twenty as she brought him into a deep, hypnotic trance. When he was even more compliant and agreeable, she began to pull of his clothes. "These clothes represent all the rules and responsibilities of society. As I pull them off you will only be left with your true self. Together we are going to explore her, and find out who she is." She stripped him naked as he sat in a hypnotic daze, allowing her to strip him completely.

"I'm going to have to ask you some questions," she purred as she strolled around him once more, the heels of her shoes clicking steadily. "If I'm going to get to the root of your delusion I need to ask you certain uncomfortable things, but you don't have to be afraid. These are not like the difficult questions women normally ask you, that you have to struggle to figure out how to answer the right way. These questions will be easy because I'm going to tell you how to answer each and every one. In fact, I'm going to make it even easier on you, and even more deeply relaxing. I know what a weak and needy little thing you are, so I'm going to do you a favor, so that you can relax even deeper. I'm going to tell you right now that the answer to every question I'm going to ask you is yes. You don't even have to think about it now. I ask you a question and the question goes deep into your mind without any resistance, because you know the correct answer will always be yes. Isn't that nice, Sweetheart?"

"Yes," John purred.

"MMM," Tanya moaned as if deeply pleased. "That's right. That's absolutely correct. I'm so proud of you."

John smiled with delight, his eyes distant.

Tanya pulled a straight backed wooden chair into the center of the room and had John sit down on it. "I love to see my pets learn quickly. I love it when they answer questions correctly. Would you like to be my pet?"

"Yes," John moaned.

"Of course you do," Tanya purred into his ear as she leaned over him. "Everyone wants to be my pet. Only a few get that honor. Only the lucky ones. Only the pretty ones. Do you want to be one of the pretty ones?" She wrapped her hand around his big, flaccid cock, gently caressing it.

"Yes," John moaned, beginning to harden in Tanya's soft, slender hand.

"Oh yes. Good pet. Such a smart pet to know the right answer to all my questions." She gently stroked his erection as she continued to purr in a soft, hypnotic voice. "I can give you that. I can make you pretty. I can make you my pet. But there is a cost. It's such a small cost, barely worth mentioning. All you have to give me is a little spot in the center of your mind. Just one little spot, the root of your mind, you might say. It will belong to me. Just open that door and let me in, and you can be everything I desire you to be. You can have the honor of being what I want you to be and doing what I want you to. Are you ready to do that? Are you ready to surrender that one tiny spot deep in the center of your mind for me?"

"Yes," John said.

"Good boy," Tanya purred. "Picture your mind as a vast dark space. Thoughts and memories are floating around it like ghosts. Now picture me. I'm walking into your mind. You can look at me all you want in here. You can look at my tits, if you like. See how the edge of my sexy red bra is showing in the opening of my blouse? Does it excite you?"

"Yes."

"I'm walking through your mind. If I wanted I could stop and take control of all the silly thoughts and ideas floating around here, but I'm not interested in this place. I'm going deeper. In the center of that space there is a door. I'm going to walk into that door and into the room at the center of your mind. When I do, this outer area, this vast space, it's going to disappear as though it never existed at all. Are you ready to let this part of your mind completely disappear?"

"Yes," John moaned, Tanya's hand moving slowly up and down his hard, throbbing cock.

"I open that door and step into a room. The vast darkness disappears behind me and it is gone forever. All those things floating around out there never mattered anyway. They never made you happy. Looking at me is the only thing that makes you happy. I'm undoing another button of my blouse, showing you a little more of that sexy red bra. Tell me about your room. Tell me about the room in the very center of your mind."

John began to describe to her in exacting detail every item and every feeling that lingered in this room. It was the culmination of all his childhood bedrooms and classrooms and his dreams of soft comfortable places.

"Ok," Tanya said. "But this is my space now. This room belongs to me. Remember, that was the deal?"

"Yes," John said, feeling like he had been somehow trapped.

"Good boy," Tanya said. She began to whisper each item in the room back to him, telling him she was getting rid of it. She made each sacred object disappear from his mind until he was left with only a blank, white room. "Doesn't it feel good to be rid of all those old things? Isn't it liberating?"

John wasn't sure, if it was liberating or not. He felt like he couldn't think at all, but then he remembered the answer to every question was yes. "Yes," he said.

She rewarded him by stroking him faster. She opened her luscious lips and let a line of spit drop from her mouth down onto the head of his throbbing cock. The spittle ran down his shaft, lubing his dick for her grasp.

"I'm so proud of my pet," Tanya moaned. Her other hand unbuttoned her blouse. She took his head and pushed it into her cleavage, letting him breath in the scent of her soft, warm body. He sat there, his face nuzzled to her breasts, his body relaxed and his cock hard and throbbing in her gentle hand. "Now we're going to fill the room back up. Picture one clear white wall in that room that I've created for you. Together we are going to write things about your true self. Now that we've eliminated the nonsense we are going to explore the true you together. Picture me standing in front of that wall. I have a lipstick in my hand. Can you see the lines of my underwear through the thin fabric of my skirt?"

"Yes," John said.

"Good boy. You can look. This is your safe place. You are allowed to look. I'm going to write something about you on that wall now. It's a deep truth that you can finally learn, now that we've gotten rid of all the clutter. I reach up, my long body stretching as I write with luscious red lipstick onto the clear white wall, 'You are weak.' Say it for me."

"I am weak."

The sound of her hand moving through the spit on his cock made it to his ears. She reached down with her other hand and gently cupped is balls. "Good boy," she said. "You are weak. But that's so sexy. Now I'm going to write another truth about you. Watch me bending slightly as I write onto the wall, 'You are a sissy."

"I am a sissy," he repeated.

"I love pretty little sissies," Tanya moaned, hand sliding up and down his meat. "Now I write another truth about you on the wall. I'm bending over, my skirt rising up my thighs and showing the tops of my nylon stockings and a hint of my red silk panties. I write the final truth, 'You're only pleasure is to serve me."

"My only pleasure is to serve you," he droned.

"Good pet," Tanya purred. "Now keep repeating everything you've learned about your deepest, truest self."

He began to repeat. "I am weak. I am a sissy. My only pleasure is to serve you."

Tanya laughed, her beautiful voice full of joy. "Yes, Good boy. Keep repeating it."

As John chanted his mantra over and over, Tanya looked at his big, throbbing cock. She was only supposed to reward him with a hand-job, but as weak and controllable as the man was, he did have a very nice cock. It felt so good throbbing in her hands.

She released his cock and hiked up her skirt. She pulled off her underwear lowering it down pat her nylon stockings. She kicked her panties across the floor. She took off her top and bra so she was only wearing her heels, stockings and her black skirt, which was pulled up to her wide, curved hips. She took his hard meat back into her hand as he continued repeating, "I am weak. I am a sissy. My only pleasure is to serve you."

She straddled his lap and hovered her wet cunt over his swollen cock-head. She slowly lowered herself down, guiding him in with one hand on his shaft and one hand and her glistening pink slit. She gasped with intense sensation as his big dick pressed into her warm cunt. She leaned against him, her tits pressing against his skin, her nipples to his, her panties on the floor, her skirt pulled up to her gorgeous, wide hips. She began to rock herself against him, working his hard prick. She placed one hand on her clit, fingering herself and the other on his back, pressing her tits against his chest as she whispered in his ear, in unison with his own mantra, "You are weak. You are a sissy. Your only pleasure is to serve me."

Her pelvis rolled and curled, rocking his meat inside her, directing it where she wanted and then grinding it into the soft walls of her wet cunt.

"I am weak. I am a sissy. My only pleasure is to serve you."

"You are weak. You are a sissy. Your only pleasure is to serve me."

The both moaned in harmony as if joined in prayer as her hips began to gyrate faster, her finger on her clit rubbing harder. She rubbed the spikes of her heels up and down his calves, her fingernails scrapping his back, her cunt rocking across his hard prick. She kissed his neck. "You are weak. You are a sissy. Your only pleasure is to serve me."

The whole chair was rattling as she began to snap her body against him.

"I am weak. I am a sissy. My only pleasure is to serve you."

Her finger worked faster, her body wiggling against him as pleasure radiated from where the fat tip of his dick rubbed deep inside her, up to the tip of her skull. She felt an intense sense of lightness as if she might drift away. She could feel vibrations moving up and down her spine and tingles running across her skin. She opened her luscious lips and purred with pleasure. "Good sissy. Good pet. Fuck! Fuck! Fuck!"

"I am weak. I am a sissy. My only pleasure is to serve you."

The orgasm caused her body to tightened and gyrate faster, a shudder of intensity shooting through her like a comet. "Fuck," she whimpered as it roared through her. "Fuck."

When her orgasm had passed she suddenly realized how close he was to an orgasm as well. His breathing was hard and his whole body was rigid. His voice was quick and frantic as he cried out, "I am weak. I am a sissy. My only pleasure..." She hoped off his lap letting his wet dick slip from inside her. She took him back in her hand and began to stroke him savagely.

"You can cum," she said. "I will allow you that pleasure, for being such a good pet. For learning your true nature."

"Thank you," he cried. She leaned over his lap, holding one of her gorgeous breasts to the pulsating tip of his cunt-wet cock. He began to fire his hot jizz against her beautiful tit. His cum sprayed all across her soft, gorgeous flesh, sperm coating her hard, pink nipple. When his balls were drained she sat back on his lap, grabbed his head with both hands and pulled his face down into her semen splattered chest.

"Eat it up, Sissy," she told him. "Eat up every drop of your reward."

He pushed his face in her perfect breast and began to lick and suck it clean of his own, salty cream. She laughed with delight as he smashed his face into her tit, eagerly slurping it clean. He suckled his own cum off her nipple as she laughed and said, "Good sissy. Good little sissy slut."

When her tits were immaculate once more she stood up, adjusted her skirt and walked over to her phone, leaving him in a mesmerized daze, cum smeared all over his stupid, blank face.

Tanya picked up the phone and spoke to her assistant. "There was a guard formerly under my employ, I'm afraid he's had an accident. Send out my condolences along with the full benefits package to his widow. Then have the island legal office print up a birth certificate for a lovely young sissy, age 25, I think I'll name her... Heather. And call in the full team of doctors. I want this one to start her surgeries right away." She hung up without waiting for a reply from her assistant. She knew every detail of her orders would be carried out.

Tanya Pain always got her way.

Asian Orphan Gurl

Tanya stood in front of the gorgeous Asian Tgirl. She looked at her, inspecting her for flaws in either appearance or demeanor. The slender brown gurl was impossibly thin, with a large, full rack. She had a flawless, feminine face and dramatic, beautiful curves. She was Tanya's favorite doll, but could sometimes be unpredictable.

The sissy doll wore a torn, brown mini-dress that resembled a burlap sack. But even wearing rags, she looked delicious. Her big, firm tits held up the rough cloth, only hinting at the incredibly trim, tight body beneath it. Her long slender legs had flawless, smooth brown skin. She had minimal makeup on, making her look even younger than her natural age of nineteen. Her body language seemed to belong to a girl too young to have the gorgeous woman's body Ting had been surgically and hormonally modified to have.

"Who are you?" Tanya asked the doll.

"Ting," she nervously answered, her dark eyes not looking up to make contact with Tanya's steady glare.

"And what are you?" Tanya asked.

"No one," Ting said. "Just a poor orphan."

"And what do you want more than anything?" Tanya asked.

"A Daddy," Ting answered. "I'd do anything for a Daddy."

Tanya moved quickly and Ting flinched as if she was about to be hit. She had been programmed to react like that, her blank, sissy mind supplanted with the powerful suggestions that made her believe she really was a desperate, needy little orphan.

"That's very good," Tanya purred. "Because I think you may be required to do quite a lot before you find a nice, rich Daddy to take you home. Do you know where you are?"

"The orphanage, Ma'am," she said.

Tanya pointed for a guard to lead the doll to the client and then she went to her desk to watch the encounter on camera.

"Well, hello precious," the tall, grey haired, white man said as he stood in front of Ting in the sparsely furnished motel room.

Ting felt his thin, brown knees tremble. He fidgeted with his tiny rag of a dress. The middle aged man leered and the pretty, Asian tranny shook. The man was older, distinguished, well-built and very handsome.

The man smiled confidently and said, "What's your name?"

"Ting," the delicate, nervous creature answered.

"Ting is a lovely name," the man's soft, strong voice rang through the room.

Ting smiled shyly, feeling eased and comforted by the man's gentle presence. "Thank you," he said.

"My name is Mr. Jones," the man said. "But you probably know that already."

"Yes sir," Ting answered.

"Would you like me to adopt you, Little One? Would you like me to take you home for this orphanage and buy you lots of pretty things?"

Ting nodded, biting his lower lip to keep it from shaking with excitement.

"Turn around, Sweetie," Mr. Jones said. "Let me have a look at you."

Ting began to slowly, nervously turn, looking back over his slender shoulder at the man. The Tranny's dark eyes burned with intensity as his heart shuddered with need, hungry for approval.

"Very nice," Mr. Jones said. "What a pretty little ass you have on you."

"Thank you Mr. Jones," Ting blushed as he turned a full 360 to face him once more.

"That dress is horrible though. You poor thing. Take it off."

Ting hesitated.

"I would love to buy you lots of pretty dresses. But I can't do that if you're still wearing that one now, can I?"

"No sir," Ting said, laughing at himself for being so dumb. He took hold of his plain, torn dress and pulled it up over his head, exposing his naked, curved little body. Ting had flawless mocha skin without a strand of hair anywhere but the top of his beautiful head. He was impossibly thin, his nutrition strictly controlled, but every inch of him was soft and smooth with gentle curves meticulously implanted or injected. He covered his slender penis with his small hand as he stood there, beautiful tits exposed. Long thin legs; full, round ass; slender, delicate ribcage expanding and contracting as his firm, artificial breasts rose and fell; pink nipples long and hard and pointing across the room at the older man. Ting didn't cover any part of his beautiful body except for his crotch, his palm concealing the tiny limp dick.

"What've you got there Sweetie?" Mr. Jones asked.

He slowly, shyly uncovered his tiny dick.

Mr. Jones laughed. "That cute little thing? Why you want to hide that from me, Sweetheart?"

"Most Daddies want their daughters to be natural girls," the tiny Asian tranny said.

"Yes," Mr. Jones said. "I suppose most daddies do. But perhaps you can find ways to compensate for your little deficiency."

"So you're naughty, and you're not a natural girl. That's two marks against you. What are you going to do to make up for being a naughty, little, sissy tease?"

Ting's hand was still caressing the man's trousers. Mr. Jones was fulling hard now Ting lovingly ran his hand back and forth over the huge, throbbing cock, just a tiny layer of fabric separating flesh from flesh. "Anything Daddy," Ting said. "I'll do anything. I'll be good or I'll be bad. I'll be your girl or I'll be your boy. I'll be anything you want."

"Why don't you start by showing me what a good girl you can be?"

Ting slid off the man's lap and dropped to his small knees on the concrete floor. He began to unbuckle Mr. Jones's belt, looking up at the man with his slender, dark eyes, big tits pressing against the older man's thighs.

Mr. Jones touched Ting's slim face with his wide hand. "Such a pretty little girl," he said.

Ting began to pull down the grey-haired man's trousers, exposing his strong hairy legs, large cream filled balls and massive, pulsating cock. Ting's mouth flooded with saliva as he felt hunger overtake his every thought. He breathed in deeply of the thick, masculine scent of the older man's cock. "Oh Daddy," he said. "I love your cock."

"Show Daddy how much," Mr. Jones ordered.

Ting looked up at the man, extended his tongue and began to lick up his pole. Ting gave a long, wet lick from the base of Mr. Jones's cock to the swollen tip, and then began to kiss back down to the balls once more. The beautiful sissy repeated the motion several times, licking a wet path up the throbbing cock and kissing a gentle path back down. The gorgeous little Asian then put his face to the man's balls and began to caress them with both lips and tongue as he gently stroked the massive prick with his soft brown hand. He breathed deeply, savoring the scent of the potent older man. "I love your beautiful cock, Daddy," Ting purred.

"Such a sweet little sissy, Ting," Mr. Jones said as he put a wide hand on the top of Ting's small skull and pulled his pretty face closer, pushing his mouth up against the big, manly balls. Ting opened his mouth wide, pressing his lips around Mr. Jones's sack. Ting sucked Mr. Jones balls into his soft wet mouth one at a time, moving his pretty face from one to the other as Mr. Jones caressed his long, silky black hair. Mr. Jones hard, fat cock was resting on Ting's smooth forehead as the eager little sissy kissed licked and sucked his fat balls.

The hard, slightly curved, somewhat monstrous cock was a striking contrast to the beautiful Asian's soft and innocent looking face.

"Such a sweet little doll," Mr. Jones moaned. His big hand ran along Ting's slender neck, possessively.

Ting moved up from Mr. Jones balls once more, kissing up his fat shaft. Then Ting opened his mouth wider than looked possible and began to slide the fat dick between his lips. "MMMM," Ting purred as the dick was washed in the warm spit of the Tranny's mouth.

"Do you like that?" Mr. Jones asked, breathing deeply as he felt the sensation of a wet, eager, sissy mouth working on his cock. "Do you like the taste of Daddy's fat dick?"

"Mmm hmmm," Ting purred as his luscious lips clamped down on Mr. Jones's hot meat and began to caress up and down. Ting felt intensely rewarded by the sound of the older man moaning with pleasure. Ting knew he was being a very good girl as he worshiped the big, fat cock. He knew he was going to earn himself a Daddy today.

Mr. Jones had one hand in Ting's deep, black hair as the other felt one of his luscious boobs, coarse skin brushing hard, pink nipples. Ting's own dick throbbed with need in his little brown lap but he ignored it. It was easy to ignore his own little cock when he had such an impressive, powerful one to use in its place. Ting bobbed his head up and down the older man's fat tool, small brown hand working the fat shaft.

"Such a good girl," Mr. Jones said. "You're making Daddy so proud right now Sweetheart."

Ting sucked harder and faster, letting the man's fat cock press down his well-trained, narrow throat.

"Oh fuck," Mr. Jones moaned. "That's a good girl. I see you've been practicing for Daddy."

The hot meat throbbed in Ting's mouth and throat as he moved his pillow-soft lips across it, washing it in gallons of spit.

"That's fantastic," Mr. Jones said. "And you are a great little cocksucker. But I didn't come all this way just to have my dick sucked. I want to feel that tight, sissy cunt of yours."

Ting let the man's fat meat slip from his wet mouth. The tiny Asian stood wiping his wet mouth as he moved up. Ting carefully and meticulously began to undress the handsome, older man until both of them were finally, completely nude.

Facing Mr. Jones, Ting moved up and straddled the man's lap. Ting planted his feet on the bed behind the older man and put his weight there. Ting balanced himself like an acrobat, ass in the air as he grabbed his own ass-cheeks and spread them wide.

Ting squatted over Mr. Jones, lowering his curved brown ass down onto Mr. Jones's massive, throbbing cock. Ting purred as hot, fat meat began to press into his tight asshole. He continued lowering his body down, letting his weight press down onto Mr. Jones's lap. Ting's asshole burned as it stretched around Mr. Jones's girth, but it was worth the pain for the deep sensation of throbbing heat that began to move inside him.

"Take my body Daddy." Ting whimpered, feeling heat and fullness as the contours of fantastic cock filled him. "Use my pretty little body. I want to be your sexy girl."

"You are," Mr. Jones moaned. "You are my sexy girl."

Ting threw his luxurious hair back, looking up at the ceiling as he whimpered with pleasure. He reached behind his feminine body and rested his

Mr. Jones began to slam his hips back and forth, fucking the little Asian sissy hard and deep, grunting with every savage thrust. Ting's body rocked across the floor with every movement, his big fake tits rolling in his tight, mocha skin. Mr. Jones grabbed one of those tits, letting his weight rest against it as he squeezed the perfect mound. Ting reached across to feel the muscles of the man's back with one hand, and reached between their sweaty bodies with the other. Ting's hand moved down his smooth, flat, sweat-slick tummy until it came to his small, raging hard-on. Ting took his own erection in his fingers and began to stroke it as that huge cock pounded inside his sphincter.

Mr. Jones grunted with every thrust and Ting whimpered. The room had an intense, musky smell. Ting's body felt full and hot and pulsating with pain and pleasure as the fat cock rammed back and forth inside him.

"You sexy fucking whore," Mr. Jones said. "I wish I really could take you home."

"You can," Ting whimpered. "I'm yours. I'm your girl, your boy, your tranny whore. Take me home Daddy."

Mr. Jones cried out and began to cum deep inside Ting's tight ass. Ting could feel the wet, warmth shooting inside him. The sensation of all that hot, creamy seed spraying into his skinny body filled Ting with an incredible, electric sensation, and he began to orgasm as well. His toes curled and his eyes closed, he bit his lips and whimpered in a beautiful, helpless way. By the time Mr. Jones second wad of filthy cum was shooting into his rectum Ting began to cum as well, spraying on his tummy and higher, squirting up against his tits as the man continued to fuck him steadily while they both jazzed in unison.

"Yes," Mr. Jones moaned. "Cum for me. Cum for me you dirty, little whore." Then he pressed his lips to Ting's and they locked into a kiss once more. Every spray of cum from Mr. Jones cock was delivered with another, brutal thrust. Both of their balls drained in unison, leaving Ting both covered and filled with filthy hot semen.

Mr. Jones sighed and rolled off of Ting, leaving Ting covered in sweat and panting for breath. Soon Ting became aware that the handsome older man was beginning to get dressed. Ting grabbed his little rag of a dress and held it in a ball in front of his shrunken little dick.

"Can I still call you Daddy?" Ting asked. "Are you going to keep me?"

Mr. Jones smiled sadly like he was going to say it was impossible, but instead he said, "Of course, Sweetie." He pulled Ting close and kissed the top of his small head. "You go have yourself wrapped up with a bow and I'll take you home tonight to join the family."

Ting jumped up and down with excitement, his tits jiggling and soft hair flowing. "Thank you Daddy," he said before he ran off towards the orphanage to go pack his things. As he got out the door a guard took him and led him back into Tanya's office.

Tanya took the little sissy by the hand and leaned over to look her in the face then whispered, "Wasn't that a wonderful dream?"

Ting's eyes lost their excited glimmer and went blank. Her body relaxed. All the childish mannerisms and body language disappeared as the little sissy became a mindless doll once more. "Yes," Ting said in a lazy drone. "It was a wonderful dream."

"Such a good girl. Such a good sissy. You can't wait to find out what you will dream next."

"I can't wait for another dream," Ting moaned.

"Good girl," Tanya repeated. She gave Ting a pat on the head and nodded to the guard who led the gorgeous little tranny back to her small, concrete cell.

Party Gurls

This was Trever's first time at the corporate retreat known as The Dollhouse and he was a little bit nervous. He had heard some crazy stories about the things that went on here, but he was sure they all had to be exaggerated. He had just made an important promotion and the fit, thirty-five-year-old executive was looking to celebrate. He didn't really know what that celebration would involve, but his boss, Mr. Bant was known for his crazy parties, and he had handled all the details. All he knew was there was a party and his "Dates" would come get him at his room.

Trevor was muscular with a tan contoured back and rugged face. He had short blonde hair and deep blue eyes and stood just over six foot tall. When the doorbell rang, he was just finishing the buttons on his silk dress shirt. He came to the door and was amazed when he opened it.

Wearing skin tight party dresses and smiling with strange, vacant eyes were two gorgeous girls. One was a blonde with a pretty face and flawless body. Beside her stood an Asian with impossibly large breasts for her tiny frame.

"I'm Jen," the cute little blonde told him, "And this is Ting." She looked at the Asian girl who bowed slightly and giggled. "We're your date for the party tonight."

"Oh yeah? My date? And just how much are you willing to do for me, blondie?"

"Anything," Jen said in a vacant, musical voice. Something about her strange tone made Trever believe that perhaps she really meant it.

"Come inside girls," Trever said. "I hate to be early to parties."

The girls both smiled big, bimbo smiles as they walked into his room. Once inside he pulled the little blonde close to him, her body soft and yielding but firm and perfectly tight. He let his hands explore her generous curves as he listened to the soft sound of her purring with excitement at his touch. He took the zipper at the back of her skin-tight party dress and began to open it. She looked up at him, her eyes soft and compliant, her curly blonde hair framing her beautiful face. As he undid the zipper she began to shimmy out of the dress, rubbing herself against him like a kitten as she peeled it off. She stood there in pink lace bra and thong, her amazing body pressed against him as he turned his attention to the little Asian.

The Asian girl stood there waiting patiently, smiling vacantly. Trever gripped her slender neck with his wide hand and pulled her to him, roughly kissing her luscious lips. Ting seemed to melt into him, her hands caressing him as he kissed her. On the other side of his body the little blonde pressed herself close, her hands also exploring.

Trever turned and kissed Jen then told her, "Why don't you help your friend out of that dress. We don't want to ruin the pretty little thing before the party even starts now, do we?"

Jen shook her head and stepped back from him. He looked at her tight body once more. She had long thin legs that were highlighted by her 8-inch silver heels. She had a slender, exposed ribcage and a tiny little tummy, but full, firm breasts. She had a gorgeous face and she smiled as she turned her attention to Ting.

Trever stepped back and began stripping himself as the two girls took each other in their arms and began to kiss. Their tits pressed together as their lips touched. Trever realized the girls had the same sized breasts, but the Asian's long, skinny body made hers look huge. The blonde began to kiss down the front of the Asian's body as she worked the zipper down the front of her dress. As she revealed more and more of Ting's supple, mocha skin, Trever got harder and harder.

He was completely naked now, watching as Jen peeled the dress down to the floor. Ting stepped out of the dress as it collapsed to a heap on the floor, wearing her black, spike heels. She wore a black thong and was already taking off her bra, freeing those firm, perfectly round, brown breasts. Jen stood up and let Ting reach behind her and free her from her own bra. Once again, the girls pressed their bodies together, breasts flattening and pink nipples pressed against one another, panties touching, hands on each other's soft, curved asses. They kissed, wet, pink tongues exploring each other's pretty mouths; deep red lips pressed together.

Trever had never seen two more perfectly built women. Clearly, they had both had some cosmetic surgery. He marveled at the clever way they had covered up the scars. On their flat little tummies, they each had vivid tattoos of little fairies in different conditions of bondage. He was staring at those tattoos when he noticed something else.

As the two girls pressed their crotches together, panties rubbing as they kissed, it became clear they weren't exactly girls at all. Poking out of the top of each of their thongs was the little purple head of a small, swollen erection. Their small erections pressed and pushed against each other as they kissed and squeezed each other's flawless, feminine asses. Trever stared in stunned silence as the two miniature hard pricks rubbed against each other in and out of the tight thongs they wore. He could see those little penises flex and throb as the beautiful trannies kissed passionately with wet, eager mouths. Their little, tranny dicks, like their perfect tits, smashed up against each other as the gyrations of their tight, horny bodies caused them to rub against together. He could hear them softly purring.

Trever couldn't believe what he was seeing. Their small dicks were shocking, but somehow still strangely feminine. "What are you?" he asked.

They both stopped kissing and turned to face him, unashamed of their slender, curved bodies, luscious tits and tiny erections. "We're yours," they said in unison.

Trever looked at Jen, "Finish stripping your friend," he said, his surprise overtaken by hunger. She dropped to her knees and began to peel Ting's thong down her slender, brown thighs. The small erection was hovering right in front of Jen's face and Jen purred over it, "Look how hard her clitty is, Daddy."

Trever couldn't help but look. The tight, flawless Asian had a completely soft and hairless body. The tiny balls and erection were not threatening at all, they were cute and strangely still somehow feminine. It was impossible not to think of the small prick as a clit. "Kiss it," he ordered.

Jen took the Asian's slim dick between her fat, red lips and began to suck it gently. Ting whimpered softly with pleasure, one hand on her enormous tits as the other caressed Jen's beautiful blonde hair. They both looked back at him as he began to stroke his big, swollen cock. Both Tranny's had their gazes locked on Trever's massive, throbbing dick as if they were hypnotized by its power. Jen's lips moved back and forth along Ting's prick and Ting whimpered softly with pleasure, but it was Trever's throbbing cock that filled both of their small, sissy minds.

Trever could see the hunger and desire on their pretty, makeup covered faces, but he could also see something else in their gazes: Deep, overwhelming envy. Some deep part of them, untouched by whatever had happened to make them into these perfect little dolls, still wished they could have somehow been real, powerful men instead of the pathetic little slaves they were destined to become.

"Come here," he told them with a rough, growling voice. "Come here and worship this cock like the dumb little sissy whores you are."

Like mindless little robots they crawled towards him, curved asses wiggling in the air, tits gently swaying, mouths slightly open and drooling, eyes locked with awe on his huge hard-on. They crawled slowly and tantalizingly towards him, Ting completely naked, Jen in nothing but her little thong, small erection poking out the top. Trever gently stroked his fat cock for them, holding it in front of their unwavering gazes like a hot, vein-crossed prize.

They reached his feet and each began to kiss his toes. They kissed up the flesh of his strong, hair covered legs, kissing past his knees to his muscular thighs, their eyes locked on his hard cock the whole time. Finally, their faces were level with his fat prick and they began to kiss it on either side. They looked into each other's pretty eyes as they kissed all the way up his shaft to his swollen head then back down, soft lips on either side of his throbbing meat. The eager little cock slaves kissed their way down to his balls, teasing and tickling them with their luscious lips and little pink tongues.

Trever reached down and put a hand on each of their heads, feeling a handful of thin silky black hair and another handful of soft, blonde curls. The tranny sluts each filled their mouths with one of his hairy balls, sucking gently.

"Tell me what you think of it," Trever said, his hard cock hovering over their small, beautiful faces.

"Amazing," Ting said.

"God-like," Jen purred.

The two trannies seemed overwhelmed with the power of his beautiful cock as their small erections pulsed in their slender laps. By unspoken agreement they each reached a hand across to the other's hard-on and clasped it between their forefinger and thumb, stroking it as they kissed Trever's fat, masculine balls.

Trever smiled. "You filthy little sissies were put on this earth to serve superior cocks like mine. You understand that right? You understand you are nothing without a real man's cock to serve?"

The two breathtaking trannies nodded, eyes fixated on Trever's massive dick. Trever's hand tightened in the Asian tranny's hair and guided her mouth up towards the head of his fat, throbbing cock. Ting stretched her mouth open wide and gazed up into his eyes as he guided his hot meat between Ting's soft, luscious lips. The tiny Asian looked like a circus freak as she easily swallowed the massive erection, her throat bulging as Trever's cock moved back and forth.

Jen had no room to kiss Trever's balls now that Ting was swallowing his massive cock, so the little blonde Tranny moved around behind the muscular Alpha male and began to kiss his ass. The two little sissies stroked each other's hard-ons with nimble fingers as their mouths worked on either side of Trever's body. Ting's mouth stretched around the fat cock that pumped down her tiny throat as Jen softly kissed her way down the crack of Trever's ass to his hairy, brown hole. Jen breathed in deep of the musky, manly scent, then extended her tongue and pressed it into Trever's asshole. She eagerly French kissed Trever's tight ass as the tiny Asian eagerly swallowed his cock. They both stroked each other's cute little penises, Jen's thong pushed down to expose her narrow erection.

Trever sighed as the sensation of those two wet mouths filled him with pleasure. He'd been blown by two girls before, but he'd never had creatures as desperate and full of need as this before. "Good whores," he said. "Good little sissy whores."

His words seemed to excite them more, or at least make them work harder. Ting's luscious lips moved up and down his throbbing shaft, caressing the contours of his cock with their pillowlike softness. Jen's little pink tongue extended deep into his tight brown hole, eagerly licking inside him; darting in and out of his asshole with quick, wet licks. Their hands moved over each other's laps, stroking each other with increasingly jerking movements as they became more and more excited. He could feel the soft firmness of their artificial tits pressing against both sides of his thighs as their mouths bathed him in warm saliva.

In front of him, the little caramel colored tranny bobbed her head, swallowing the thickness of his hard, throbbing meat between her spit moistened, hormone softened lips. Behind him that magazine perfect blonde ate his asshole like a starving, dead eyed slave-girl. Trever grabbed each of them by their luxurious hair and held them firmly as he began to pump his hips, moving his cock deep into the Asian sissy's throat one moment, then grinding his asshole back into the blonde's eager mouth the next.

Spit ran down his balls and the crack of his ass while the two tranny slaves worked tirelessly to please him. He moaned with pleasure, his hands caressing their hair, gazing down at Ting's soft, beautiful face as it stretched around his fat cock. Ting looked up at him with compliant, submissive eyes. The gorgeous Asian had the tiny frame of a young village girl, but the full, drastic curves of a porn star. Trever's heart was pounding as he looked her up and down. He'd never seen a more perfect body. He'd never believed a creature this flawless could exist.

"Eat it, whore," he said. "Eat my cock like the brainless little sissy slave you were born to be."

She offered no complaint or dispute as she stared up at him, her throat bulging with the movement of his fat cock. Trever pumped his hips faster. Harder and harder his dick plunged down the small, Asian sissy's esophagus as the blonde worshiped his tight, brown hole with her pink, darting tongue and soft wet mouth. Trever grunted, hands wrapped in their lustrous hair, saliva washing over his body. His legs began to shake and his toes began to curl up off the floor.

"Fuck," he grunted. "Oh, fuck yes."

His hips began to tremble and he started losing control of his body, no longer humping their pretty, hormone smoothed, surgically enhanced faces. As his body froze in shaking ecstasy, the two sissies took over for him. The Asian moved her small face back and forth with quick, jerking movements, plunging his dick deep down her throat. The blonde bobbed her head against his ass, sliding her sloppy wet tongue deep inside him, tongue fucking his ass like it was a delicious, tender fruit.

Trever jerked back on Ting's hair, pulling till her pretty face was hovering inches in front of his dick. The two sissies jerked each other's small erections as Trever took his hand off Jen's head and began to stroke his own, massive, throbbing cock. Ting held her mouth open wide, pink tongue extended, eyes obedient and waiting. Trever savored the feeling of Jen's tongue pressing deep into his asshole as his balls tightened and he began to spray hot cum on the gorgeous Asian's face.

Ting pressed her free hand over her own throbbing erection, covering up like a shy girl as the feeling of hot semen splattering her face sent her over the edge. Her dick, still being jerked by Jen's smooth hand, began to spurt off, filling the palm of her little brown hand with sticky white cream. Wad after wad of hot, white jizz shot onto her pretty, Asian face as Trever's balls unloaded. She whimpered and extended her tongue even more as every hot jet hit her soft, caramel skin. Jen's tongue was buried deep in his asshole as his body shook, shooting the last few drops of sperm into Ting's open mouth.

Satisfied, Trever stepped out from between them and looked down at them. The two tranny's gazed lovingly into each other's eyes. The Asian was spent, her chest heaving as she caught her breath, face covered in semen, the palm of her hand cupped and full of her own cum. She still stroked the little blond, who's own hands now cupped her tits, squeezing them as her little sissy friend stroked her thin, throbbing shaft.

"It's okay," Trever told the little Asian. "You can finish off your little friend."

Ting smiled gratefully, her cum splattered face glowing. She leaned forward, moving her gorgeous head over Jen's slender lap. Jen moaned, her big tits heaving as she breathed deeply, savoring the sensation of her friend's wet mouth swallowing her erection. Jen took Ting's cum filled hand and guided it with both hands up to her gorgeous, pleasure filled face. As Ting's head bobbed over the pretty blonde's lap, Jen held the Asian tranny's palm to her mouth and began to lick the cum from it.

"You're so delicious," Jen purred, licking Ting's palm with long strokes of her soft tongue. "I've never tasted anything as beautiful as you."

Ting's head bobbed faster, eager to make her pretty, little friend cum.

Jen whimpered in a high-pitched voice, her head tilting upwards, back arching. Ting reached her spit wet hand down Jen's long, slender neck, tracing her way down to one of her gorgeous tits. Ting squeezed gently as her luscious lips slid up and down Jen's slim pole.

"Yes," Jen whimpered. "Oh yes." Her skinny, tight body began to shake as orgasm overtook her. She began to spray her own cum into Ting's eager mouth. Ting swallowed every drop of the little blonde's semen, then sat up, smiling beautifully. Jen leaned forward, passionately clasped Ting by the hair and began to lick Trever's filthy cum from her face.

"I love you," Jen said as she eagerly slurped the semen from her friend's beautiful face. "I love you."

"I love you too," Ting purred, kissing her, filling her mouth with her own, salty cum. They kissed until they grew tired then they lay down on the floor, holding each other in their thin, feminine arms. Trever left them there to go get himself another shower before the party.

As they lay basking in the afterglow of their orgasms, Trever began to shower and dress, eager for the two little sissies to escort him down to the party. The two trannies held each other, cuddling and breathing in soft unison. Soon they began to whisper to each other about their dreams of escape.

In her office, watching on camera, Tanya Payne laughed. She thought their ideas of freedom were comic and adorable. She spread her long, gorgeous legs and moved her hand up her slender thigh, sliding it under her skirt. She pushed her panties to the side and pressed her finger to her wet cunt. Tanya shuddered with pleasure as she thought about how the two, mind controlled sissy dolls would never be free of her power.

Tanya fingered herself as she watched the two dolls shimmy their slender, curved bodies back into their skin-tight party dresses. They looked submissive, compliant and eager as they stood by the door, holding hands and waiting for their man. Tanya caressed her own wet cunt as she watched them standing there, faces vacant and eyes full of stupid happiness. Suddenly her tall body rocked with thrilling orgasm. She moaned with ecstasy as the pleasure radiated through her, thinking about how her silly little dolls would always belong to her.

Silly Sissy Dreams of Freedom

Jen watched as Ting walked up from the beach carrying a handful of fish she had trapped in the retreating tide. She wore a little pink bikini. The mocha skin of the slender, Asian transgender shimmered in the sunlight. Her large breast threatening to slip out of the tiny bikini top with every breath, she walked towards the little cabin, letting the air dry the tiny drops of water that glistened on her brown skin.

Jen couldn't quite remember when he had met the breathtaking Asian doll, but his feelings for her were overwhelming. Jen could feel the nipples of his own large breasts hardening, even as his small penis hardened, pushing against the fabric of the tight silk slip he wore as he stood in the cabin looking out at Ting. Jen knew that, to Ting, he also looked like a gorgeous woman, a beautiful blonde with crystal eyes and bright skin. Jen idly touched his big breasts, his hands always wanting to take in the reassuring beauty of them. He let his hands slide down his smooth, slender body, feeling his curves as he grew more and more excited, watching the gorgeous Asian's tight little body sway deliciously as she walked up the pathway to the cabin.

Jen's heart fluttered with anticipation. How long had Ting been out? He couldn't remember. His mind didn't work right anymore. Once he had been a normal man. He understood that but didn't remember it. He had been living some distant, unremembered life then one day he had been turned into this, beautiful doll. He had escaped from the compound where he had been changed through surgery, hormones and mind control, but he couldn't remember how he escaped, or even why, exactly, except that Ting had wanted to.

The door opened and Ting walked inside. The gorgeous Asian Tgirl smiled at him, illuminating her beautiful face as she set her fish on the counter and moved forward into his arms. The two stunning tranny dolls began to kiss each other passionately, pink lips pressing together as soft hands explored the curves of each other's soft, feminine bodies. Ting was hard, her small, thin erection poking out of her tiny, pink bikini bottoms. Jen reached down and wrapped his hand around the Asian beauty's slender brown rod, stroking her gently as he kissed her soft lips.

Their tongues wrestled in each other's wet little mouths as their hands cupped the other's tight round asses, long, thin backs glistening in the sunlight. Jen's erection tented the soft, silk slip he was wearing and Ting reached under it with both hands, gently fondling his small, hairless balls as she softly stroked his small penis. Jen's sweet, feminine voice purred as the pleasure of the sissy doll's gentle touch sent shivers through his small, thin body.

"Make love to me," Ting purred.

They both stood, stroking each other's hard erections as they gazed into each other's beautiful eyes. Jen leaned forward, his tits pressing against Ting's tits as he pressed his lips to hers and began to kiss her.

"Starting without me?" Michael said as he gazed at the two, gorgeous transgender dolls kissing and stroking each other. He stood in the entryway to the bedroom, wearing nothing but a loose, black pair of swimming trunks.

They looked back at him as if surprised to see him there. Jen smiled, suddenly remembering the man who had helped them escaped. He was almost 60 and slightly overweight, but to Jen and Ting he seemed like the most beautiful man they'd ever seen.

"Never without you Daddy," Ting said.

"We owe you everything," Jen purred.

From her office in the compound, Tanya Payne smiled. She loved watching her dolls play out this particular scene. Tanya had decided that the best way to destroy her little sissy's dreams of escape were not to suppress them, but to use them. She made the doll's most desperate dreams into her own, highly marketable fantasies. She had designed this fantasy to twist their desperate little dreams into her own, deliciously wicked playthings. She had designed the scenario and put it on the menu for men who didn't come with her own fantasies. It was called, "Fugitive Lust" and it was proving to be a very popular option. Already her favorite little sissies had played the roles out a dozen times with a procession of different men. Soon, when they dreamed about escaping from Tanya Payne's Dollhouse, they wouldn't even be able to imaging making it farther than this little cabin just outside the compound.

Ting and Jen held hands as they approached Michael. Jen's heart surged with awe for the powerful, older man, and love for the gorgeous Asian tranny. The two sissies' slender, curved bodies swayed as they approached the older man. They got close and he wrapped them both in his arms, kissing them one at a time as the other nibbled on his neck.

"Thank you so much for helping us escape," Jen purred.

"We owe you everything," Ting agreed.

"You are so welcome, little ones," the older man said with a wicked smile as his hands explored their flawless, hormone softened skin.

Ting stood on her tippy toes and whispered into Michael's ear. "Jen was about to make love to me, Daddy. Would you like to watch?"

Michael smiled. "I can't imagine anything more adorable than that."

Ting smiled at Jen and the two, gorgeous sissies leaned across the older man's chest and pressed their luscious red lips together. They moaned in soft, tantalizing voices as they began to kiss. Their little pink tongues darted in and out of each other's wet mouths as their hands caressed each other's generous curves. Ting took Jen by the hand and Jen's heart began to flutter as the gorgeous Asian led him to a small bed in the corner of the cabin. Michael stood watching as Ting took Jen in her arms once more and kissed him gently.

"Make love to me," Ting purred.

Their soft, artificial breasts flattened against each other as their lips locked and their tongues entwined. Ting took hold of Jen's slip and pulled it up over his head, leaving the gorgeous little blonde standing there in only his pink panties, tiny erection poking out the top. Ting stepped back and admired her beautiful blonde friend. Ting untied her bikini top and let it fall to the floor. Jen stared at the gorgeous Asian doll's amazing breasts, pink nipples hard as pencil erasers. Ting took hold of her bikini bottoms and shimmied as she peeled them down her slender brown legs.

Ting backed onto the bed, looking up at Jen with her dark, mysterious eyes, her small, thin hard-on throbbing between her skinny, mocha thighs. Ting brought the fingers of one hand to her lips and began to suck, slobbering wetly. Ting laid back and purred as she pressed her glistening fingers to her ass, gently probing herself.

Jen listened to Ting's lustrous moaning as he peeled his panties down his long, model-slim legs. Jen crawled onto the bed and pressed his soft, surgically enhanced body against Ting's flawless frame. Jen pressed his lips to Ting's nipples, sucking them as he guided his small, hard rod to Ting's spit moistened asshole. Jen could feel Ting's erection, throbbing against his flat little tummy as he pushed his dick into Ting's willing asshole.

Ting purred as Jen buried himself inside her. "That tickles, Sweetie," she said. Jen rocked his body back and forth, his dick hot and hard in Ting's soft ass, as his tummy rubbed against Ting's tiny throbbing erection. The sensation of Jen's soft flesh pressing against Ting's dick as it lay pressed between their bodies, as well as the sensation of Jen's prick tickling her rectum made Ting moan softly. Jen cupped Ting's beautiful tits as he kissed them eagerly, rocking back and forth against the gorgeous, Asian tranny.

From the doorway, Michael took out his big, hard cock and began to play with it as he watched the two trannies make gentle love.

Ting purred in Jen's ear, "You've got me so turned on, my love, but I need a real cock to get me off."

They both looked back at Michael with hungry need in their pretty eyes.

"Daddy," Jen whimpered. "Will you come fuck us please. We need your beautiful cock to get off."

Michael stripped as he walked to the bed. He moved on top of the two sissies as Jen wiggled on to the gorgeous young Asian. Michael let his weight smash down one the two Trannies. He grunted into the little blonde's ear, "Spread your cheeks for me, little slut."

Jen reached back and spread his supple ass cheeks wide with both of his small hands, his small cock still buried deep inside Ting. Jen felt the incredible weight of the man, pressing him even tighter against the soft, curved body of the breathtaking Asian doll. Jen let his face burry in Ting's ample chest as Michael pressed the swollen head of his fat cock against Jen's trembling, brown hole.

Jen felt his body relax as the fat, purple head of the man's beautiful dick touched his quivering flesh. He felt his body prepare itself as his soul yearned to be filled with hot meat.

Michael pressed his hips forward and Jen whimpered in a broken little voice as his asshole was split open by the man' fat, throbbing cock.

Michael sighed as he let his prick invade the slender blonde sissy. He moaned as his dick was squeezed by the soft flesh inside the little tranny's tight sphincter.

Jen rolled his soft curved ass back against the man, then rocked forward into Ting's asshole. Jen knew Ting could barely feel his thin erection inside her, but the feeling of the Asian's tender hole felt incredible on his needy little prick. Jen reached back up and held Ting's gorgeous breasts once more, pressing them against the sides of his pretty, makeup covered face.

As the older man's big cock was pressed back and forth deep inside Jen, he felt an incredible feeling of fullness and purpose radiate from inside him. Jen could feel the man's hot pulse thundering inside him through the veins that bulged from the man's impressive meat. Jen's soft, high pitched voice whimpered with every thrust of the man's hips, driving his soft body tight against the slim, mocha tranny.

"How's that feel," the man grunted. "How's it feel to have a real man's cock inside you?"

"Good," Jen whimpered. "So good, Daddy." The feeling of fat, sweaty dick invading him made Jen's whole body vibrate with hot, pounding pleasure even as his violated rectum ached with pain. Faster and faster the man began to pump his cock inside the little blonde tranny, and harder and harder the pulse of that pleasure moved in Jen's slender little frame. Every thrust of the man's hips sent Jen smashing down into the impossibly slender Asian Tranny, his hard-on burying inside her delicate brown hole. Every gyration of Jen's impaled body rocked the hormone softened skin of his tummy against Ting's throbbing erection.

Again and again that magnificent, fat cock pummeled deep inside him to the music of his own high pitched whimpers and Ting's soft purring. The pain became merely a dull ache in the background as the pleasure grew and grew.

"I love it Daddy," Jen whimpered. "I love your big, beautiful cock."

"You were born for this," the man grunted. "You were born to take big dicks in your tight little sissy ass."

Jen knew it was true. He didn't know how he got here, or what he was before he became this model-perfect blonde whose slender body and soft curves thrilled both real men's cocks and his own needy little erection, but he knew this is what he was always meant to be.

Jen cried out as his ecstasy intensified to an unbearable level. Pleasure seemed to explode deep inside him as a powerful anal orgasm overtook him. Jen's small, hairless balls tightened as he began to shoot his hot, sticky load into Ting's soft, willing asshole. Ting giggled with pleasure as thick waves of sissy sperm shot into her rectum. The man still pounded Jen's ass, his weight almost suffocating as pleasure made all Jen's limbs stretch out beneath him. His slender back arched and he cried out, "Fuck yes, Daddy. Fuck yes. It's so good. It's so fucking amazing."

Soon the orgasm passed and Jen went limp and relaxed as the fat prick continued to slide back and forth inside him.

Jen looked back over his small, feminine shoulder and begged the older man to, "Please fuck my lover now Daddy. She needs a real cock inside her too."

Jen groaned as Michael pulled his huge cock out of his sphincter, leaving him feeling like there was a raw and tender void inside him. Jen slid up to kiss Ting's luscious lips, his raw, pummeled ass still throbbing with heat.

Michael knelt between both trannies's skinny, spread open legs and pressed the head of his beautiful hard-on against Ting's hole. Jen's cum dripped from Ting's brown opening, making her slick and ready for the strong, older man's much larger pole. Jen spun around and sat on the cushion of Ting's magnificent tits, leaning over so he could see the man's massive prick split his lover open.

As the older man's cock began to slide into Ting's body, Jen could see Ting's small erection twitch and dribble precum. Jen's mouth watered and he leaned lower, taking the slender Asian tranny's skinny brown dick into his mouth. Jen looked at Ting's thin, caramel legs, her tiny ankles braced against Michael's shoulders.

Ting whimpered with a sweet, submissive voice as the fat cock began to press deep inside her, and Jen's luscious red lips moved up and down her throbbing prick. The man wrapped his fingers around Ting's surgically enhanced hips, marveling at the curve to her impossibly skinny waist. Jen slurped loudly as he washed Ting's dick in wet saliva, twirling his tongue around her sensitive flesh.

Ting purred, "Your mouth feels so good. It feels almost as good as Daddy's fantastic cock."

Jen could see that fantastic cock sliding in and out of Ting's gorgeous body, her soft ass cheeks flattening against him with every thrust. The memory of that cock moving inside of his own asshole filled Jen's slender body with sympathetic pleasure. He felt like he could still feel it, pulsing and radiating warmth inside him. Jen drooled saliva down Ting's prick as his pretty lips moved up and down the hot, thin shaft.

Jen's slender body had already brought the man close to the edge, and now he pumped Ting ruthlessly as he grunted with a need for release. Ting's delicious whimpers filled the room as her dick began to twitch in Jen's wet mouth. The man pounded the little Asian harder and harder as Jen sucked her faster and faster. Jen's head bobbed, blonde curls bouncing, tits jiggling, as his weight held Ting steady for the raw, primal fucking her slender brown body was receiving.

Jen listened to the savage grunts of the man and the musical whimpers of the tranny as his wet mouth slid up and down Ting's slim pole.

"Fuck," Ting cried. "Fuck Daddy! Your dick is so good! I feel you so deep inside me! I'm going to cum! I'm going to cum from your beautiful cock!"

Again and again Michael slammed that beautiful cock deep inside Ting's sphincter. Ting finally lost the ability to form words, her luscious lips making only high, animal sounds as her balls tightened and her body trembled and radiated with heat. Jen felt Ting's delicious sperm begin to spray into his eager mouth as her whole body went rigid and her arms squeezed tightly around Jen's waist.

Jen swallowed down mouth full after mouthful of salty warm jizz as Ting's body shook and writhed with ecstasy.

Ting relaxed with a deep sigh and began to shower Jen's ass with hundreds of tiny soft kisses.

Michael pulled his cock from Ting and pressed it to Jen's lips as Jen let Ting's limp cock drop from her mouth. "My turn," Michael said.

Jen spread his mouth wide and let the huge, magnificent prick slide between his spit moistened lips. Michael grunted with pleasure as he felt the softness of Jen's wet mouth engulf him.

Jen let the massive cock fill his mouth and slide down his throat. He looked up at the powerful, older man with deeply submissive, grateful blue eyes. Jen wanted to thank the man for helping them escape. He wanted to thank the man for being so clearly superior to the two little sissies, but still blessing them with his big, throbbing cock. He wanted to thank him for even noticing them. Jen couldn't speak with the fat cock in his mouth so he thanked him by sucking harder, humming as he slid his luscious red lips over the ridged contours and bulging veins of the man's impressive meat.

Michael groaned and grabbed a handful of Jen's blonde hair, caressing the sissy's skull. Jen gazed up at the man, slurping on his cock, eager to taste the contents that swam in his big, hairy balls. Michael's breathing increased and his weight shifted. Jen had no idea how many men's cocks he had sucked in his life, but he had no doubt that this one was about to cum.

Jen slipped the fat rod out of his throat and out of his mouth. He held the glistening cock inches from his open mouth as he stroked it with both hands. He gazed up at the man with hunger in his pretty, blue eyes as he let his little pink tongue lap at the bulging purple head.

"Fuck yes," Michael said. "You beautiful, stupid little whore. Get ready to eat my cum."

Jen was born ready as he spread his mouth wide, tongue extended hands stroking faster.

The first wad of hot, salty cream shot deep into Jen's open mouth. He opened wider, thirsty for more. Thick white semen splattered Jen's tongue, lips and chin as Jen stretched his lips even wider, and extended his tongue out even farther. Jen stared at the rewarding pleasure in the man's face as he unloaded every drop of filthy cream from his balls into Jen's wet mouth and onto his pretty face.

When Michael was done, and finally sighed with release, Jen closed his mouth and swallowed the delicious reward he'd been given. Michael sat down on the bed, looking relaxed and content while Jen turned and pressed his soft, curved body against Ting's.

"It feels so good to be free," Jen sighed as he snuggled into Ting's arms.

"Yeah," Ting said, but she had a strange look in her eyes, as if she didn't quite believe it.

Jen put his palms on Ting's cheeks and turned her face to his, then gave the gorgeous Asian tranny a tender kiss with his cum filled mouth. Ting's mouth came alive as her body filled with passion once more. She squeezed Jen's soft, round ass as she drove her tongue deep into his mouth.

With Michael watching beside them on the bed, and Tanya watching on the monitors in her office, Ting rolled on top of Jen, pressed her small erection to his quivering asshole and made soft, sweet love to him.

The Elfish Waif

John drifted out of a trance. Time felt strange and he wasn't sure where he was, or even who he was, but he felt like he had been strapped to this medical table for months and months on end. He could vaguely remember another life as a security guard at an island for feminized sissy dolls, but he wasn't sure if it was real or a dream.

He looked at the nurse beside him. She wore a tight little uniform that flattered her slim, sexy body. "Help me," he said.

"What do you need doll?" the slender brunette asked as she raised his platform, bringing him to a sitting position.

"Food. I'm starving."

"I'm afraid you're simply not capable of eating solid food anymore," the nurse said. "The operations you've had on your stomach make it impossible for you to be feed any other way then by IV. I'm afraid any meal bigger than a mouth full of sperm will cause you unbearable pain." The nurse laughed at the sissy's expression. "I know. It's more severe than most of our girl's dietary regiments, but Tanya had a very specific vision for you. Elfish waif is her word for it I think... Don't look so sad sweetie, I'd gladly take those operations if I thought they'd make me look like you. You're getting all your nutrients from the IVs. Don't worry, there is a team of doctors regulating every drop. Just look at how much it's paying off."

The nurse turned John's chair so the tall, slim sissy could see his new body. The hormones, the operations the lotions and oils applied hourly to his skin and hair had all done their job. The six-foot tall sissy looked like a red-haired, pale skinned movie star. He had been shrunk to bone thin, but anywhere bone would have shown through his tight, supple skin, soft curves had been surgically implanted. He had firm, proud and natural looking C-cup breasts that stood out from his trim frame, hard pink nipples pointing in front of him.

The nurse giggled at his reaction. "What did I tell you," she said. "The boss is a true artist."

John thought he was going to hyperventilate with shock, but he couldn't help but be amazed by his own long, feminine body. He had miles of slender legs, soft and supple skin, with luscious dark red hair framing his pretty, pale face. His lips were full and pouting, his lashes long and flirty, his nose small and petite. If he saw this girl on the street, he would be afraid to talk to her. His dick was getting hard as he stared at himself, realizing he was actually in possession of a beauty that terrified him.

The nurse stared at his big, hard cock. "Fuck," she purred. "You are certainly well-built for a little sissy." She leaned over him, placing one hand on his hard cock as she whispered into his ear. "I'd love to play with it, please."

John was still staring at himself in the mirror and didn't answer, but the nurse wasn't really asking for permission. The nurse moved in front of him and knelt between his long, thin legs. She took his big dick in her mouth and began to drool over it as her head slowly rode up and down his shaft.

John stared at his reflection. With the slim nurse's head bobbing up and down in front of his crotch, there was absolutely nothing in that reflection to say he wasn't a beautiful woman instead of a feminized sissy doll. The nurse's saliva dripped down his shaft and washed over his hairless balls, dripping down the crack of his soft, curved ass. The nurse made slurping noises that filled the room as she hungrily sucked on him.

John closed his eyes, the sensation of that eager, wet mouth beginning to overwhelm him. "Oh fuck," he moaned, surprised by the sound of his soft, feminine voice. "Oh fuck, that feels so good. Oh yes."

The nurse slurped up and down his shaft, her soft lips pressed against his throbbing meat as if she was starving to consume him.

"Oh yes," John purred. "Oh yes." His tits heaved as his breath grew quick and heavy. He closed his eyes, bit his lip and clenched his fists as the pleasure built higher.

Suddenly the nurse stopped sucking him. She stood up, ignoring his spit-wet erection now as she straitened her tight little uniform and prepared to leave.

"What are you doing?" John asked.

"I'm all done," she said, checking her reflection in the mirror, fixing her lipstick.

John stared at the panty-lines in her skin-tight uniform, longing to touch her and be in her mouth again. "Please don't stop," he begged. "I'm so close."

"I know Sweetie. I'm sorry. Ms. Payne said I could play with you, but I'm absolutely not allowed to let you cum."

"Please," John begged.

The sexy young nurse laughed. "Sorry. I'm not about to disobey Tanya Payne. Trust me. She's not someone you want to piss off." She looked at him, sympathetically, his hard-on throbbing and his hands strapped to his chair. "There is something I can do for you," she said. With that, the nurse turned up the levels on the drug's in John's IV and let him slip back into a delirious, trance-like state.

Sometime later, hours or perhaps months, Tanya Payne was standing in the cell of her newest sissy, looking him up and down.

Tanya Payne looked at the gorgeous young sissy. His surgeries and physical treatments could not have gone better. The slender, six-foot tall man had been starved beyond skinny, while all his jagged places had been injected or surgically modified to be soft, feminine curves. His hair had been grown out past his shoulders and dyed a beautiful, dark red color while his skin had been softened and lightened to the quality of fine porcelain. His breast augmentations were very natural looking, giving him a nice, curving profile. His long legs were exquisite before Tanya's team of specialized doctors had even begun their series of surgeries and hormone treatments.

Physically, Heather was flawless, but mentally, he still clung to his resistance. He still clung to the idea that his name was John, and that he was capable of making his own decisions and forming his own thoughts.

Tanya circled Heather. The tall, thin tranny was naked, strapped to a medical table, staring up at the ceiling with drugged over, trance filled eyes. Again, Tanya admired her new doll's big, fat dick as it hung limply in the thigh gap between his narrow, pale thighs.

"Hello there, little one," Tanya purred.

"Hello," Heather droned in a distant, vacant voice.

Tanya dropped warm oil onto her palm and pressed down Heather's feather soft skin to her limp dick. She grasped that beautiful cock and began to gently caress it. "Are you ready to be my pet?" she asked.

"I don't understand what's happening," Heather complained, as he searched within the depths of his brainwashed mind.

"I didn't ask what you understand," Tanya said firmly. "I asked if you're ready to finally become my pet."

Heather's eyes swam up from emptiness and focused on Tanya's beautiful face. "You're so beautiful," he said. "I just wish I understood what was happening. I don't remember anything."

"You don't remember because there is no room in your pretty, little mind for useless things," Tanya purred as she slowly stroked her oil filled hand up and down Heather's hardening shaft. "Before I found you, you were only a useless thing. I had to erase all those useless memories and ideas to make room for the ideas I wanted you to have. Now you are a beautiful thing. A beautiful, valuable toy for me and my friends to play with. Isn't that nice?"

"Why are you doing this?" Heather pleaded as his rock-hard cock began to throb in Tanya's grip.

"Because I want to," Tanya said. "Because it's what you need. It's what you deserve." Her oil-slick hand made soft, squishing noises and it stroked up and down Heather's prick. She reached up with her free hand and turned up the level of drugs coursing through his system, sending him falling back into a deep, suggestive state.

Tanya waited a while, gently stroking Heather's rock hard cock as she studied his gorgeous face. Finally, she spoke once more. "You haven't been forced into this fate; not really. You've been drawn to me by something deeper. Your whole life, the world has lied to you. It has told you that you're something you're not. It's told you that you can be someone you can't. It's told you that it's better to pretend to be what you can never become then to be you're true, natural self. It's told you to suppress your, soft, weak, beautiful nature and try to act like one of the big, strong men whose very presence makes your balls tremble with nervous energy and desire to please and placate and submit. You fear it, but your soft, weak nature is what makes you so beautiful. Your tender, compliant heart is what makes you such a wonderful toy. You don't have to fight it, Princess. Not here. Not in this place. This is your home, where you truly belong. You weren't captured, not really, not if you think about it really carefully. If you think about it real carefully, relaxing your mind and letting my voice chase away all your silly and insignificant thoughts... you will finally remember that you were drawn here. You came here on your own, begging to be made into this because you couldn't quite do it on your own... remember?"

"Yes," his voice droned. "I remember."

"Good girl," Tanya purred, smiling with triumph as she continued to stroke him. "That's such a good girl that you finally remember. And if you try... if you relax even deeper, you'll remember how good it feels... how absolutely amazing it feels... to give in to your deep, sissy nature. You'll remember with perfect clarity, the incredible pleasure of giving up the illusion of manhood, and no longer clinging to your desperate little ego."

Looking into his face, she knew he could feel it: the thrill of surrendering to that intense sensation. The thrill of no longer struggling against the submissive, needy little bitch inside him. Tanya felt something inside him breaking as she slowly stroked his rock-hard erection. "Don't fight it," she urged. "Allow yourself to feel the intense waves of pleasure that come from no longer pretending to be a man."

Heather sighed as if giving up a terrible burden.

"You can feel it now," Tanya purred. "Stronger than memory, stronger than anything you've ever felt: That intense pleasure and freedom that can only come from giving in to your natural, sissy nature. You can feel it, that blissful word, moving through you like your very soul speaking to you, saying, surrender..."

"Surrender," he moaned, his dick throbbing in Tanya's gentle hand.

"Good girl," Tanya whispered, hot breath against his ear, running across the tiny hairs at the back of his slender neck. "Say it again,"

"Surrender," he said breathlessly. "Surrender."

"Good girl," Tanya said again. "I'm going to let one of the guards fuck you now. It's going to hurt, but you're going to love it. You're not going to love it because it feels good. You're going to love it because I'm going to love it. You're going to love it because he's going to love it. You're going to love it because other people's pleasure is more important than yours. Other people's pleasure is more important than your pleasure, your happiness or your self-respect. The more of these things you surrender to me, the happier and sexier you are going to be. Are you ready to be mine, Little Fuck Thing? Are you ready to surrender everything to me?"

"Surrender," he purred.

Tanya pushed her lips to his ear as she let her hand slip from his throbbing cock. She purred into his ear, "If you are a good girl, and you make my guard very, very happy, I'll even let you finish. I'll stroke your big, sissy clit until you cum all over my hands." She held her hands in front of his face, allowing him to imaging them dripping with hot, filthy cum. "Would you like that? Would you like to be rewarded like a good, obedient pet?"

"Yes," Heather moaned. "I want to cum so bad."

"If you want your reward, you have to pay the price. But that's okay, you will learn to love the cost." Tanya stepped back and nodded to the guard who stood waiting in the hallway. He stepped into the room. He fastened a steal collar attached to a length of chain to Heather's long, pale neck. He held Heather's leash of chain as he unfastened the slim sissy from the table. The guard guided heather forward. He led Heather to a buckle that was built into the floor and clipped the short leash onto it, forcing the slim, naked tranny to bend forward, head lower than ass. Heather began to kneel but the guard slapped him across the pretty, pale face.

"Straighten those legs, whore," he ordered in a deep, growling voice.

Heather straightened his long, pale legs and extended his slender arms pressing his palms to the floor for balance.

Heather was tall, and had exquisitely long legs. The guard was tall too, but not quite tall enough. "Spread your legs," the guard ordered.

Heather's slender ankles swayed as the frail sissy let his feet slide apart.

"Wider," the guard barked, slapping Heather's soft pale ass sharply, leaving a deep red handprint.

Heather whimpered weakly as he spread his legs wider, bringing his ass to the right level.

Tanya sat down on the medical table, crossed her long, tan legs and smiled as she watched the guard begin to finger Heather's tight, virgin ass. Heather whimpered, his oil slick dick still hard. Tanya watched the guard's fat fingers probing Heather's tender hole for a minute that she told the guard, "That's enough foreplay. She's a sissy, not a princess."

"Yes Ma'am," the guard said. He unfastened his duty belt and let his uniform slacks fall to the ground. He took his fat erection in his hand and pressed it to Heather's quivering hole. One hand gripping the virgin tranny's pale flesh at the hip, the guard guided his hot prick, pushing it into Heather's tight opening.

Heather whimpered in pain as the guard's swollen purple head pushed its way inside him.

"MMMM," Tanya moaned, sitting tall with her hands crossed on her bare knee, just beyond the hem of her skirt. "I love that sound. That delicious whimper the first time a little sissy has her ass claimed."

The guard drove his cock deeper into Heather's tight rectum, making the tranny cry out with pain, defeat and humiliation.

"Good girl," Tanya purred. "When the pain gets too much, just remember your reward. Imagine how good it's going to feel to finally have that release. Are you picturing it?"

Heather's eyes were closed as he groaned with ass splitting pain. "Yes," he said, his dick still hard and dripping with oil. "Yes, I'm picturing it."

The cock buried deep in Heather's tight asshole, then slowly began to withdraw. Both hands on Heather's curved hips now, the guard moaned with pleasure.

"Imagine my hand, sliding up that slippery toy between your legs. Imagine the pleasure you will feel as I own your toy like I own the rest of you. As

I play with your sissy clit like I play with the rest of you, like I allow the rest of you to be played with."

Heather groaned as hot, throbbing cock moved back and forth in his tender, virgin sphincter. He looked at the gorgeous blonde vixen out of the corners of his eyes as he grunted.

"Tell the guard to fuck you harder," Tanya commanded. "Tell him you love it when he hurts you."

Heather whimpered. "I can't take it any harder."

"Of course you can, doll. Your pain does not matter. Pain is the cost of your release, but only good girls get rewarded. Show me what a good girl you are."

"Fuck me harder," Heather grunted, surrendering to his deeper need. "Please. I love it when you hurt me."

The guard laughed softly as he squeezed Heather's pale flesh tighter and began to fuck him harder. The sound of skin slapping against skin, the guard grunting and Heather whimpering was like music to Tanya's ears.

"Don't worry, my precious pet," Tanya said. "You will learn to enjoy it eventually. For now, just know that I enjoy it. That should be enough for you, but if it isn't yet, you can imagine your reward. I give you permission to imagine my hand, making your body finally have the orgasm you've been denied for so long."

Heather stared at Tanya's breathtaking body as his body was hammered back and forth by the guard's powerful hands and big cock. Soft red hair bouncing, tits jiggling, hard-on flopping, Heather's body was pounded relentlessly. Tanya watched with a beautiful, wicked smile. "Tell the guard you love his cock inside you," she said.

Heather's voice was weak and wavering with suffering as his slender new body was ruthlessly violated. "I love it," he whimpered. "I love having your beautiful cock inside me."

The guard slammed his dick deep inside Heather's rectum with savage thrusts, drool dripping from his contorted mouth onto Heather's pale, slim back.

Tanya Payne stood up and walked towards the brutalized sissy, her heels tapping on the floor. She stepped up close and took Heather's throbbing erection into her hand once more. "Good girl," she purred as she began to jerk his oil-slick cock.

Heather gasped as if Tanya's touch was a revelation. As the cock slammed deep inside him, his own penis was already close to exploding.

Tanya laughed. "Such an eager little pet," she said. "I barely have to touch you, don't I? That cock inside you has you so turned on. It hurts, but it's remaking you. Your soft flesh is bending around it and your becoming something new. My beautiful pet, my eager toy...." She stroked him faster as she felt his body move closer and closer to ecstasy. "You can't even tell the difference anymore can you? My hand on your cock, the cock in your sissy-cunt, it's all just one sensation, one throbbing pounding need filling you with pain, pleasure and the promise of release. Surrender to it little fuck-thing, surrender yourself away to me."

Heather's long thin legs began to tremble and his frame began to shake. He grabbed his own slender calves as if afraid of losing himself completely while the orgasm raged through him. Tanya cupped her hands over his cock, no longer stroking him as he began to fire hot jizz into the palms of her beautiful hands.

The guard, rocking back and forth, pounding his fat cock inside the little sissy's gorgeous ass, grunted as he too began to cum. Hot sprays of semen fired deep inside Heather's sphincter, intense and powerful like a firehose. Heather's luscious lips formed strange, passionate shapes as he silently mouthed his pleasure and pain. The guard pumped a few more brutal thrusts, making Heather's slender body rock back and forth as he emptied the contents of his balls in the sissy's soft, round ass. The guard sighed with release and let his dick slide out from inside the elfish waif of a transgender doll. He stumbled back and leaned against the wall, catching his breath.

"Good girl," Tanya purred. She raised her sperm covered hands, glistening in the light, and held them to Heather's beautiful, sweat covered face. "Time to clean up, little doll."

Heather hesitated and Tanya said more firmly, "You don't expect me to clean up after you, do you?" She pushed her cum dripping hands closer to Heather's face with insistence.

Heather spread his luscious red lips, extended his little pink tongue and began to lick his cream off Tanya's soft, beautiful hands.

Ganged in the Guard Barracks

Heather stood at the door looking at the beautiful blonde mistress who had taken complete control of his mind, body and life. He wanted to hate her but he couldn't. He was mesmerized by the slender, six-foot-tall vixen's beauty and he was thrilled by the amazing power she exerted over him. Him? Was that even an accurate way to describe himself anymore?

He could see his reflection on the polished steel wall just past Tanya Payne's gorgeous figure. He was gorgeous as well. Also standing six-foot-tall, he stood even taller in his spike tip heels. He had long, dark-red hair and a thin, willowing frame. He looked too graceful and flawless to be real, but he was. Wasn't he? He had gorgeous curves and delicate features and perfect, pale skin.

He wore a little black summer dress that sat lightly and his little curved frame. His deliciously long legs seemed glow a lustrous white. His heels made his already perky little ass sit even higher, his slender back curved, his chest pushed out. His tits looked full and proud on his slender frame, pointed nipples pushing out the light fabric of his dress. He wore no bra, but his tits stood high and tight against his narrow chest. Under his dress he wore a tight, pink thong, his big dick bulging, but locked in limpness by a small steel sheath that had been fastened over it and attached to his shrunken, hairless balls.

The little chastity tube kept his dick compressed, uncomfortably shrunk to half its size, and he kept shifting his body to try and relieve the uncomfortable sensation.

Tanya Payne smiled at him, which, despite all the cruelty she had showed him, filled his heart with eager joy. "You look delicious, little sissy," she said.

"Thank you," he said, hating the sound of his desperate, needy voice.

Tanya stepped closer and caressed Heather's slim arm with her long, delicate fingers. "Normally I'd program a doll a whole new identity for something like this. I'd go into your weak little mind and twist it around until you believed you were a hooker or a virgin or a lost little doggy, but I thought it might be fun, just this once, to let you have your memories. When I let you into this barracks room, you will recognize all the faces, remember all the names and feel all the old familiar feelings, but deep down, you will still belong to me, and you will still be powerless to do anything but fulfill my filthy desires." She paused, letting her seductive voice reverberate down Heather's spine. "Would you like to fulfil my filthy desires little pet?"

Heather nodded eagerly, even as his heart trembled with fear. He knew exactly where the door they were standing beside led.

"When I open this door, you will recognize all your old work friends from security, but they won't recognize you. To them you will just be a filthy doll, a dirty little toy that belongs to me. You do belong to me, don't you Sweetie?"

A deep part of Heather wanted to turn and run. He couldn't remember his old name or his life before the island, but he could remember working with all these men, standing among them joking and telling stories, pretending to be a man. But a deeper part of him knew he had always belonged to Tanya Payne and that to disappoint her would be the most terrible failure he was capable of. "I belong to you Ma'am," he said.

"Good girl," Tanya purred, then opened the door to the security barracks.

As Tanya strolled into the room, tall and graceful and commanding, her body full of luscious curves, Heather walked shyly behind her like a nervous pet. "Good evening boys," Tanya said.

Men in various states of undress rushed to cover themselves as they stood. Some men stood at attention, falling back on their military days as their rarely seen boss entered the room. Other men merely stood and watched, but everyone stopped what they were doing and gave the radiant blonde their complete, respectful attention. Tanya stopped and presented her pet with a flourish, "This pretty little thing is called Heather. She is a very nice example of the quality product this island is becoming famous for."

Heather felt humiliated as the men's stares moved over his slim body, all of them knowing he used to be a man, or used to pretend to be a man. He swallowed hard, feeling the lust in all those eyes. Even as his skin crawled, recognizing each desire filled face, his body also began to surge with heat. He didn't want to feel it, but he did. He felt a rush of excitement knowing he was wanted. As a man, he had been just another one of them, anonymous in the crowd, barely worthy of talking to. As a transgender doll, he was the center of attention and the object of their interest. His dick was tingling, which made him breathe deep. He focused, trying to keep his dick from growing in the tight little tube and causing him pain. He tried not to look at the men and instead stared down at the floor. He wondered why Tanya felt the need to humiliate him like this, but, of course, she wasn't anywhere near done.

"You men are doing a great job," Tanya said. "I have decided you deserve a reward. I'm giving you Heather." Tanya smiled wickedly as she looked back at Heather's gorgeous, terrified face. "You can do whatever you want to her. She is very sturdy, so I doubt you'll break her. If you do, she can easily be fixed or replaced. Enjoy."

Heather was trembling like a leaf. Even staring at the floor, he could feel the lust filled glares of all those familiar men moving over his long, feminine body.

"Enjoy," Tanya said. "I'll send someone around to collect her in a few days."

Tanya turned smartly on her heels and began to stroll elegantly away. As she passed by Heather she hesitated for just a moment. "Remember all I taught you, Little doll," she said in her hypnotic, sensual voice. "Remember how good it feels to surrender."

The word "surrender" seemed to echo deep in Heather's mind, brushing against some long forgotten primal urge that lived deep inside him. His towering, feminine body felt like it was flooding with warmth and tingling electricity, even as his heart pounded and his lips trembled. He looked across at the sea of familiar faces, all turned unfamiliar with wanton desire. However long it had been since Heather had been one of them he had been transformed. His legs were thinner than most of these men's arms, even though he stood taller than most of them. He stood taller than every single one of them with the treacherously high heels he stood trembling in.

The men closed in on him, their eyes red with lust and their lips wet with saliva. Heather swallowed hard and turned to the barracks door, staring at Tanya's delicious frame as she slipped past the threshold, imagining at any moment that she would turn back and rescue him. She did not, and the door closed behind her with a heavy click that rang with finality.

Heather took a deep breath and closed his pretty eyes, long eyelashes delicately entwining. Hands began to grope him. Rough, calloused hands touching the flesh of his skinny legs and arms. Fingertips caressed his face and hands squeezed his firm, artificial breasts through the fabric of his dress. Finger's pinched his soft, feminine ass, voices laughing at his whimpers.

He wanted to tell them to stop, to beg them, but deep inside him that word continued rolling through his broken little sissy mind. "Surrender," it said in Tanya's compelling voice. "Surrender to your weak, sissy nature."

Heather breathed deep, his dick aching as it tried to get hard in the chastity device. Hands roughly pinched, squeezed and slapped his flesh. He could feel his nipples getting hard as the men began to rip off his dress. "Surrender." Tanya's voice wiggled in his brain, whispering "Surrender." His body was surrendering, whether he liked it or not; nipples like pencil erasers, hard and sensitive, lips parting, voice moaning softly and hormone softened skin tingling as he was groped by uncountable hands.

The dress tore away from him, leaving his statuesque form exposed to eyes and hands. He wore only the panties and soon they were torn away too, leaving him with only his elevated heels and his chastity device for adornment. His dick ached as it tried to fight against the metal tube to swell. Even soft the restrictive tube was uncomfortable, his big, limp cock compressed to the size of a shrunken worm, but as it tried to swell with blood, the pain was agonizing.

Rough, masculine hands gripped his delicate pale flesh as he was lifted off his feet. He whimpered with fear and with an unexpected and undeniable thrill; he was now totally under their power. They placed him on his hands and knees like a dog, whimpering on the dirty floor as hands continued to pinch and squeeze his sensitive flesh. Men surrounded him and towered over him. He felt like he was at the bottom of football, dogpile, helpless and trapped in the depths of a wall of strong, male flesh.

Despite the terror and claustrophobia that surged inside him, his body also pulsed with expectation and need. "Surrender," Tanya's voice seemed to whisper. "Surrender to the bitch inside you."

Heather cried out when the first cock penetrated his slim, feminine ass. Heather didn't know if he was a virgin or not, the time he had spent being conditioned and trained by Tanya Payne was a dreamlike blur, but the pain of the hard, throbbing cock that was splitting him open was undeniable. "Fuck," he whimpered. "Oh fuck. It hurts."

No one cared. Hands kept squeezing and pinching as a huge erection was pushed against his soft, lustrous lips. Heather opened wide without hesitation or question, his body working without his permission. As the fat prick pushed into his wet mouth he greeted it with his tongue, caressing the underside like a loyal pet, eager to please. Eager to surrender.

"Surrender," Tanya's imaginary voice was louder in his mind than any of the real sounds that surrounded him. The men grunting and laughing, the saliva sloshing as fat cock pumped back and forth in his wet little mouth, the sound of thick sweaty dick sliding back and forth in his tight little asshole; it all sounded distant and faded compared to the tantalizing sound of Tanya Payne's voice, burrowing through is skull. "Surrender little bitch. Surrender to the power of real men."

Heather whimpered into the gag of fat, anonymous cock as his colon was violated with hard, eager thrusts. The pain racked through him like an electric shock. He couldn't tell which sensation was more torturous, the aching pain of his ass being impaled, or the sharp pain of his cock trying to get hard against the cold steel chastity device. The cocks pounded back and forth on either side of him, filling both his holes with throbbing heat. Heather's body suddenly took over, and he began to feel it surrender even deeper.

He relaxed and, though the pain didn't disappear, he felt a certain kind of pleasure, fluttering deep inside him. He imagined his new, sexy body, kneeling at the men's feet. He knew he was probably the most beautiful creature any of them men had ever touched. Most of these rough, calloused men never imagined they could have a gorgeous thing like Heather the doll to play with.

Heather arched his back, trying to make his body look even more tantalizing for them, feeling the thrill of their lust filled eyes touching him as much as their strong, eager hands. The cock in his ass was pummeling deep inside him, shattering his helpless body with waves of pain and slowly intensifying pleasure. Suddenly the cock was buried to the base in Heather's body and began to spray his rectum with hot, slick cum.

Heather could feel his own, soft prick leaking precum as his asshole was filled with wave after wave of hot jizz. The cock in his mouth began to slide back and forth, pressing against his throat and making him gag as hands held tight to his deep red hair. The cock in Heather's ass slipped from him, leaving his aching sphincter stretched and pained. He felt relief and loss as the fat prick left his anus hollow. It only lasted a second though and another fat prick was shoved deep inside him.

The dick between his supple red lips began to twitch in his wet mouth and Heather knew instinctively what would happen. The man groaned and began to fire hot jizz into Heather's mouth and down his narrow throat. Heather swallowed it down in thirsty gulps, his whole being flushed with pride as he tasted the thick, salty cream.

"Surrender," Heather thought in her own, feminine voice. "Surrender to the pleasure of others. Give in to the power of real men and stop fighting what you were always meant to be." He slurped down mouthfuls of sperm and saliva as the cock continued to press back and forth in his mouth. His raw ass ached with pain and throbbing hot pleasure as the cock inside his ass hammered back in forth in his cum-drenched hole. His asshole felt silky smooth as an unseen but familiar man pounded his sphincter with savage thrusts and slobbery grunts.

As the softening cock was pulled from his mouth, three others pushed forward to take its place, pushing against each other and pressing against his face they fought for dominance until one triumphed and slipped into his soft, open mouth.

Cock after cock came inside his mouth and ass only to be replaced by new tubes of meat. Heather lost count of all the throbbing sweaty dicks that invaded his body, pumping him hard and fast and cumming quickly inside him. He began to feel like he was connected to some exotic fuck machine, pounding him brutally at both ends. The pain had become so intense that it somehow turned into something else. It merged with the pleasure that was growing inside his slim, feminine core. The pleasure and pain wrapped together and throbbed in harmony to the dicks and the hands and the lust filled eyes. It grew and grew as cock after cock impaled him.

"Surrender," Heather thought. "Surrender to your true, sissy nature." His toes began to curl and his legs began to quiver, his arms were rubber and his balls were tightening. With a fat cock moving inside both his holes, Heater's body began to burst and shiver with orgasm.

His limp, encapsulated dick began to shoot cum out the tiny hole at the tip of his steel tube as the men at either side of him began to fire more globs of sperm inside his mouth and ass. He felt that hot jizz moving inside him as his own semen spilled to a little puddle on the floor between his long, splayed open legs.

Soon the cocks stopped filling him and Heather crawled to his old cot and curled on the floor beside it. His body pulsed and radiated with the afterglow of his deep and intense orgasm. He felt fundamentally changed and deeply ashamed as he savored the taste of cum on his tongue and felt it dripping out of his ravaged asshole.

A man sat down on the cot beside him and Heather looked up at the familiar face. "You?" Heather said, searching his dim little mind for the man's name.

"Hi, fucktoy," he said back, laughing softly.

"Greg," Heather pleaded. "It's me. I don't remember my name, but you know me."

Greg laughed. "I think I'd remember you little whore."

"No," Heather begged. "I was your friend. I was in the bunk beside you. That one right there."

Greg moved closer, hovering over him as he stared into Heather's eyes, ignoring his gorgeous hair, pouting lips and soft, lightened skin. "John?" he gasped. "Holey shit, it is you. They said you died, almost a year ago."

"You have to help me out of here," Heather said. "You have to help me escape."

Greg laughed. "You don't really seem like you want to escape. I haven't heard you turn down a fucking from anyone yet. You seem to fucking love it like a dirty little whore."

Heather wasn't sure she liked the tone in Greg's voice. The man still hovered over him, his weight and body language dominant and full of desire. "I can't help it," Heather said. "She did something to my mind. I see cock and I just... I just can't resist it."

Greg laughed. "You know why I was your friend? You used to always show me pictures of your pretty, little wife. I couldn't wait to fuck her. I did too. She barely mourned you for a week before she was ready to have me shove my fat cock in her." Greg hesitated, his dark eyes drinking Heather in. "She was nowhere near as hot as you are though."

Greg pulled out his fat cock and held it in front of the pale, redheaded sissy. "Tell me you don't want it," he said. "Tell me you don't want it and I'll take you out of this place."

Heather swallowed the saliva that was flooding into his mouth. "I don't want to want it," he said.

"You don't want to want it but you do. You don't want to need it but you do. I'm glad the boss captured you. You were always a sissy bitch." Greg grabbed Heather's waifish body and flipped him onto his stomach.

Heather whimpered as the man's weight fell on his slim, sissy frame. Heather felt the heat of the man's iron hard cock pressing against the soft flesh of his round little ass. "Please," Heather begged.

"Please what?" Greg growled.

Heather's body was trembling and full of heat. He couldn't fight it anymore. "Please fuck me like you fucked my wife."

Greg laughed above him, his voice thick with scorn. Heather didn't care. He needed that cock inside him. He needed to feel the warm acceptance of the man's hot cum splattering against his flesh. "Please," he begged again. "Please fuck my little sissy ass. I need it so bad."

"How many times you been fucked tonight?" Greg asked.

"I don't know, but I still crave more."

Heather gasped as he felt Greg's thick cockhead burrowing between his soft ass-cheeks. He pushed his ass up, pressing it towards his old friend, begging with his body language to be penetrated by the man's throbbing, hot meat.

Greg groaned with pleasure as he took Heather's raw, ravaged but willing asshole.

Other People's Toys

Eddie shifted his tool bag in his hand. He had a temporary keycard to get him through the security doors in this maze of a compound but it didn't seem to be working anymore. He had worked later than he planned. This job would take weeks, so he hadn't been trying to finish it in one day, but sometimes you just couldn't stop your work until you reached a certain point.

He scanned his temporary keycard again and got another red blinking light. Perhaps his authorization had expired, or maybe it was something wrong with this door. He stared at the heavy steel door that led back out to the lobby and sighed with defeat. He turned around and started wandering the dark hallways, looking for another way out.

He had never been to this island before. They had called the 37-year-old electrician in to fix some generator problems. He loved to travel the money was good, but this place made him nervous. He knew it was a resort for rich people, and he imagined there was a lot of prostitution that went on at a place like this, but he had heard rumors of mind-control and slavery. It was easy to dismiss them all as nonsense in the light of day, but down here, in the darkened concrete corridors, wandering lost, it was a little harder to ignore. Everywhere he went he came to keycard readers that his keycard wouldn't open, so he kept wandering, trying every door until one opened.

He walked into a hallway that ran down a series of small rooms. The space had a different atmosphere than much of the utilitarian compound. Although the outer walls were still raw, grey concrete, the wall separating each room was clear, spotless glass. Although lit by dim emergency lighting now, it looked like the place would be bright and somewhat cheery with the regular lights on bright. There was strange equipment everywhere. The area looked like a cross between a black-market medical clinic and a very advanced beauty salon. Not a soul was visible as he walked down the corridor.

About halfway down the hall he glanced through the glass of one of the rooms and noticed someone or something laying on the examination table there.

His first thought was that it was some-kind of incredibly lifelike doll. Part of his mind told him not to be so curious, but he couldn't resist getting a closer look at the incredible, beautiful thing. The lifelike blonde looked like it was modeled after a movie star or a flawless lingerie model. The doors to these rooms didn't even have locks and he stepped through the glass and walked up to the gorgeous form. The blonde apparition was laying perfectly still, open eyes staring blankly at the ceiling. His first shock was when he saw the tiny dick hanging between the gorgeous blonde's slender thighs. The second shock was when she turned her face and stared at him with vacant, expressionless eyes.

"Are you here to take me back to my cell?" she asked in an expressionless voice, as if it was no concern to her if she was in a cell, or laying on the hard examination table staring blankly at nothing.

"Who are you?" he asked. "What are you doing here?"

"I'm Jen," the strange, beautiful blonde said. "I am here for my scheduled skin treatments and cleanings. But those are all finished. Did they forget to put me away?"

He looked at her exquisite naked body and then felt a tinge of guilt for staring. He took off his uniform shirt, standing in just his undershirt he held the blue, button down top out to her. "Do you want to cover yourself?" he asked.

She seemed to think about that for a moment, as if searching the deep recesses of her memory. "I haven't been told to want anything yet. Do you want me to want to cover myself?"

He looked at her supple skin, gorgeous tits full and firm, tiny ribcage and sunken tummy, shrunken little waist and full, curved hips. He had never even seen a woman as beautiful as her before... If he could even really call her a her... The shirt dropped from his hand. "No," he said. "No I don't want you to cover yourself."

"What do you want?" she asked.

"I want to touch you," he said, his voice almost pleading as if it was a request that would certainly end in rejection. He stepped closer, his fingertips twitching at the thought of feeling her flawless young skin.

She looked at him with a vague look of expectation on her otherwise blank face. "I was made to be touched," she said.

He wasn't sure if she was giving him permission or not, so he tentatively reached forward, brushing her side with his fingertips slightly to gauge her reaction. There was none. Her beautiful, blank face was completely unaffected.

He reached up and cupped one of her breasts, staring into her thoughtless eyes. The soft flesh of her firm breast felt like silk against his sweaty palm. He felt his cock stirring in his pants. He wondered if all the rumors of strange mind-control drugs and hypnosis were true after all, or if she was incredibly advanced robot.

"Are you... Did you used to be... real?" he asked.

"I don't know," was her distant, droning answer.

"You're fucking amazing," he said. Feeling bolder now, he touched her with both hands, caressing her perfect young flesh, trying not to look at her small cock. It was the only imperfection in her otherwise flawless, feminine body. "Can you... cover up your dick?" he asked. "Put your hand over it or something?"

"I don't understand," Jen said blankly. "Is that a question or a command?"

Eddie swallowed and steadied his voice. "A command," he said.

Jen took one of her slender hands and covered her crotch with it, completing the illusion of being a flawless young girl. His hard prick was uncomfortably pressing against his slacks as he felt the soft, pliant body in front of him. He finally let his hands slide from her gorgeous young flesh and brought them back to his uniform trousers, unbuttoning them and letting them fall to the floor. He lowered his underwear and stepped out of his clothes, standing naked before the little doll-like blonde. She had no reaction. Not a hint of shock or disgust showed on her flawless young face.

Eddie took his hard, throbbing cock and pressed it to Jen's luscious red lips. She just lay there, staring at him as his dick pushed against her closed mouth, not showing the slightest reaction. He took his dick and slapped it against her cheek. Still she stared vacantly. His dick was harder than it had been since he was a much younger man. He slapped it against the pretty blonde's face again, much harder. "Come on," he pleaded. "Open up."

At the command, she opened her mouth wide, holding her lips spread like she was waiting for a doctor to inspect her tonsils. Eddie took a deep breath and pushed his cock in. She still laid there, mouth stretched open as he slid his dick around in her wet palate. It felt fantastic, but it was strange, she wasn't doing anything, not even closing her lips around his hot, throbbing shaft. He took his fingertips and pressed on her chin, closing her mouth, but still she did nothing as he slid himself around in her soft, little mouth. "Come on," he said again. "Suck it."

Suddenly she came to life. Her head lifted from the exam table and her body turned to its side as she began to slurp hungrily on his meat. Her head started to move back and forth, lips tight against his skin. It was as if he had found her 'On' switch. He could feel the warm saliva filling her mouth and streaming down her lips as she moved her head back and forth, slurping loudly. The hand that wasn't covering her small hairless penis was reaching up and cupping his balls, gently caressing them as she sucked him. Her empty blue eyes gazed up at him as he reached down and began to fondle her perfect breasts once more. He could feel her nimble tongue working around his pole as her soft lips slipped tightly up and down his hot, throbbing flesh.

"Oh fuck," he moaned. He'd never been sucked so expertly before. The truth was, he couldn't remember the last time he was sucked at all. "Good girl," he said. "That's a good girl."

The vacant little doll seemed to react again, as if he had found the switch to turn her up a level. Her head bobbed faster as she sucked him harder, purring with what sounded like pleasure as she ate his meat. He couldn't help but sneak peeks down at her crotch, the small hand covering the little penis like a shy girl covering her tight, pink pussy. Eddie began to rock his hips, pumping into the little blonde's mouth in time to her bobbing head. He had never felt such an intense feeling of wet suction or such a thrilling sensation as her little pink tongue dancing across his prick.

He closed his eyes and groaned. He was close, just a few more bounces of her gorgeous blonde head, just a few more thrust of his hips, and he would be spraying his hot semen down her throat. He thought about how eager the little doll seemed. He supposed she would have to be. Without a pussy, the little tranny slave would be used to taking cock down her throat and up her...

Eddie froze. He had never given it to a girl up her ass. How many times had he begged girls to let him try anal only to be rejected? Jen's wet mouth still slid eagerly across his pole, bringing him closer and closer to the point of no return. He reached up and grabbed her head firmly, stopping it before it was too late. "Your ass," he said in a desperate, hoarse voice. "I want to fuck your ass."

Jen's glistening red lips slipped off his throbbing meat and she looked up at him with her beautiful blue eyes. "Yes sir," she said. He stepped back amazed by her obedience. He admired her gorgeous body as she began to move off the exam table. She carefully kept her crotch covered as she slid to standing on the floor then turned away from him. She spread her legs and bent over the exam table, her hand cupping her little dick and tiny balls to keep them out of sight from every angle.

Eddie's pulse was thundering as he reveled in her eager compliance. "Fuck, girl. Do you ever say no to anything?"

"Do you want me to say no?" She asked. "I can. I can resist if you want. I can cry and scream. Would you like that sir?"

Eddie's hand cupped and caressed the curves of Jen's feminine ass. "Is that what you want?" he asked.

"I haven't been told what to want," she said. "My memories are blurry images flashing across a blank wall. My thoughts are all made of cotton candy. The only thing that is clear is I am created to serve. Please let me serve you. I have no meaning without it. Without your desire washing over me, I can feel myself starting to disappear."

Eddie spread Jen's pliant ass-cheeks and spit on her little brown asshole. He had never been harder in his life. "You don't have to fight me," he said. "It's clear all the fight has been brainwashed out of you, little whore." Despite everything, he half-expected her to protest or get offended, but she accepted his name calling as obediently as she accepted his touch. He took a deep breath and began to press his cock into her tight, round ass.

Jen's girlish whimper thrilled him as he pressed his meat inside her. His hands ran up her slender legs and traced the curve of her gorgeous hips. His hands reached her tiny waist and he wrapped his strong fingers around her, her body impossibly slender in his grip. He held her tiny little waist as he rocked his hips, moving his cock deep inside her soft, warm rectum. He pumped back and forth inside her, amazed at the sensation that came from her practiced little asshole. As he plunged forward, her sphincter muscles relaxed, allowing him to drive deep inside her. As he pulled back out, the silky flesh of her anus tightened around him, as if clinging to his hot meat, begging it to stay inside her.

Eddie began to pump harder, watching her soft ass jiggle slightly as he rocked her to and fro by her dainty waist. "Tell me how much you like it in your slutty little ass," he said.

She looked back at him, her eyes blank but obedient. "I love it when you fuck me in my slutty little ass," she said, her voice full of realistic pleasure. He fucked her harder.

"Now tell me you hate it," he said.

"I hate it," she whimpered in a venomous little voice, her blue eyes still empty as the afternoon sky. "I hate it when you fuck me. I hate your filthy cock inside my tight little body."

He continued ramming her, grunting with every thrust. She whimpered as he pounded her. Her tits pressed flat against the exam table, her blonde hair cascading and swaying across her shoulders and back. He stared at that gorgeous, slim back. He remembered a picture he had a long time ago, snipped from a magazine when he was still a kid, a gorgeous model with a rail thin, tapered little back. This back looked even more amazing. How many times had he jacked himself off to that picture? Pumping his cock as the slender blonde in the picture looked over her shoulder with a sensuous smile.

"Look back at me," he commanded.

Jen looked back at him over her tiny, tan shoulder blade.

"Smile at me," he said. "Look like you want me."

The lust filled smile that suddenly appeared on the doll-like, bimbo face amazed him. Her eyes seemed to glow with passion as her breathing increased. He pumped away at her tight little asshole, groaning with pleasure.

"I want you," she purred. "I want you so bad. Fill me up with your dick. Own me with your hard, throbbing cock."

Eddie took his own cock in his hand as he watched the beautiful t-girl play. He moaned, one hand on his fat cock. The other hand reached out and caressed Jen's blonde hair and pretty face. "Show me what an eager little whore you are," he said. "Make yourself cum. I want to watch you eat your own filthy sperm like the dumb little piece of trash you are."

The hand that caressed her cheek reeled back and slapped her across the face once more. Jen gasped with the sharp slap, as if nothing could have been more intensely pleasurable to her. Her tits rose as her chest expanded with a deep breath, her nipples hard as little pink pebbles. They stroked their cocks as they looked at each other, the little blonde's mouth wet with drool. He slapped her face again and she whimpered and her whole body seemed to quiver with ecstasy.

"That's it," she moaned. "That's it. I'm going to cum. I'm going to cum so hard."

"Catch it in your little whore mouth," he said. "Don't spill a drop."

He was amazed at her flexibility as she bent forward, her lips not far from her pulsating pink rod. He put his hand on the crown of her head and pressed her down a little more, his other hand still stroking his own cock furiously.

Jen had her mouth wide open and her tongue extended, her eyes open, eyelashes fluttering. She whimpered as she began to erupt, streams of hot jizz firing up into her wet mouth and splattering against her luscious red lips.

Eddie groaned with excitement, finally slipping over that edge. His pulse thundering and his breathing ragged, his balls tightened and he began to cum. He fired load after load of sticky cream into the tranny's radiant blonde hair as the tranny fired her own semen into her own mouth. The last few spurts of Jen's sperm had less force behind them and they shot onto her chest, and dripped down her lovely tits, funneling down her nipples and forming little drops like morning dew that landed in her slender lap.

Eddie continued to stroke himself, filling her lustrous blonde hair with his spooge like it was a filthy little cumrag. When the last drop of cum had been squeezed out of his pulsating rod, Eddie stepped back and looked at the gorgeous little tranny. She swallowed hard, her feminine throat working as she ate her own sperm. She opened her mouth so he could see that she had swallowed every drop except the remnants that had glazed her lips and dribbled down her tits. Her hair was sticky with cum that ran down and dripped onto her shoulders.

She smiled, licked her lips and swallowed the glaze. Her instructions complete, he watched her face transform once more. Before his eyes her face became devoid of feeling, looking up at him, lifeless and blank. Her hollow voice asked, "Is there anything else you desire?"

Eddie felt suddenly embarrassed and frightened. What was going to happen if he got caught playing with toys that were not his? "No," he said as he quickly dressed. He glanced around the room, wondering if there were cameras in here recording his every move. What would be the punishment for using a doll built for rich, paying customers. Would he somehow become a doll himself?

He hurried out of the room, leaving the gorgeous sissy toy kneeling on the floor, stained with cum and staring at nothing. He eventually found a way out of the compound, packed his suitcase, got the late ferry and never set foot on the island again.

Girls Love to Play with Dolls

Heather stood in front of the door to his client's room. He didn't know anything about them. He barely knew anything about himself. It was normal though. It was very common for sissies to be unable to hold their flighty little thoughts in their pretty little heads. Isn't that what someone had told him? Hadn't he been told it was best not to try? Why think when you can just wait and be told?

Heather looked down her long, thin body, checking his wardrobe. He wore eight-inch spike heeled pumps that made his height of six-foot-tall even taller and exaggerated the length of his gorgeous thin legs and the curve of his small round ass. He wore a tiny flared skirt and nylon, fishnet stockings that reached half way up his thigh, several inches below the hem of his skirt. He wore a tight denim vest that gathered the cleavage of his natural looking, artificial breasts. He smoothed out the cloth with his palms, tracing the graceful curves of his long skinny body.

The door opened and a pretty but harsh looking brunette stood at the door looking at him with cold, brown eyes. She wore elegant black slacks that flattered her petite frame and a luxurious silk blouse that hid her small, firm breasts. She looked him slowly up and down, her critical gaze tracing the contours of his slim, curved frame. "Delicious," she finally said. "Tori, the toy has arrived."

A pretty, feminine blonde hurried into the hallway and looked at Heather with eager eyes. She wore a loose, flowing skirt with a pink blouse and heels. Her soft, plump curves were a contrast to her friend's tight, angular frame. "Wow," Tori said in a sweet, ditzy voice. "There is no way that's a boy. Cath, this is some kind of trick."

"One way to find out," Cath said. She moved forward, pressing her slender body against him. She reached under his skirt and grabbed his limp dick through the lace of his panties. She was not gentle as she squeezed him, her nails biting into his flesh. Heather cringed and whimpered at the sudden, roughness touch.

Cath laughed. "A certified boy," she said to Tori then purred to Heather, "Sorry, Sweetie, am I hurting you?" she taunted without releasing any pressure on his throbbing dick. "I'm not used to handling the real thing. It's usually rubber and silicone for me and my lovely wife."

Tori held out her hand, presenting her ring. "Newlyweds," she said. "I have the sexiest, most wonderful wife in the world." She smiled adoringly at her dark-haired bride.

Heather tried not to cry out, Cath still gripping his prick like she wanted to punish it.

"I'm also rich," Cath purred into Heather's ear. "So rich I can afford to change a man into a little transgender plaything if I want. I was thinking of finding a stupid young boy and having him shipped to a place like this and converted as a wedding present to my sweet, wife. But I must do my due diligence. I have to try one out before I have one made." She looked at Heathers face and added, "I am sorry I hurt you earlier." She was still hurting him.

Heather whimpered, "It's okay Ma'am," even though she hadn't released her tight grip, choking his shaft and drawing blood with her nails.

"He's so pretty," Tori said, blue eyes wide with amazement. "I wish all boys looked like him."

Cath finally released Heather from her iron grip and put her arm around the bubbly little blonde. "If you like it I'll have one made for you. A pretty little sissy slave to cook and clean so you don't have to worry about anything but being my pretty little trophy wife."

Tori giggled, her plump cheeks flushed with heathy color, her tiny pug nose making Heather want to fall in love with the adorable blonde as well.

Tori looked at him curiously, then she asked her wife, "Can I see it? Can I see her dick?"

Cath smiled at Heather. "You heard her slave. Show my sweet little wife the toy she gets to play with tonight."

Blushing, Heather pulled up his skirt. He rolled the waistband of his panties, inching them down then slid his big, limp dick out the top. Tori giggled. "She's as big as that strap-on I like. The one you got for Valentines."

"Okay Slave," Cath said. "Put that filthy thing away till were ready to play with it. Come with us, I think my wife would like a foot-rub."

Heather pulled his pink pace panties back up and followed the two girls into the main room. The two women swayed gracefully as they held hand hands. They sat down on the couch, still holding hands. Cath crossed her legs and sat proud and tall, looking at Heather like he was an unwashed peasant girl. Tori kicked off her heels and rubbed her cute little feet against each other. Heather's gaze fixed on those beautiful feet as they brushed together, smooth, tan skin delicious in the soft light.

Heather knelt, his flared skirt raising to show his panties and curved little ass as he dropped leaned forward and took one of Tori's beautiful feet into his soft hands. Cath's hand caressed the lower thigh of her cute, blonde bride as she watched Heather caress the arches of the woman's delicate feet.

Tori purred, a smile of pleasure on her pretty face as Heather's fingers eagerly massaged her.

Cath gave him a sharp little kick in the shin with the tip of her shoe and then gave him a dirty look. "Use your mouth too, little bitch. I should have to tell you everything."

"Sorry," Heather said then leaned forward and pressed his pink lips to Tori's flesh.

"Oh," Tori said. "Don't be mean to her sweetheart."

"Shhh," Cath said soothingly. "Don't worry your pretty little head about the feelings of a slave, my love. You just enjoy and leave its training and punishment to me."

"Of course, your right Sweetheart," Tori said. "Sorry."

Cath leaned over the blonde and they pressed their lips together. The two pretty lesbians began to kiss as Heather ran his little pink tongue across the arches and between the toes of Tori's gorgeous little feet. When they finished there sweet and passionate kiss Cath leaned back and said to her wife, "Would you like to have sex with the little slave?"

Tori nodded, "Are you sure. You won't get jealous of her?"

"It," Cath corrected. "And no, I will never get jealous of a little sissy slave. Why don't you go change and I'll make sure it's ready, okay?"

Tori nodded and stood up, giving Heather a flirty smile before hurrying into the bathroom.

Cath stood up and said, "Come with me, bitch." She turned and walked into the bedroom. Stopping in front of the bed the small brunette began to strip. She pulled off her slacks, top and bra, kicking off her shoes until she was wearing only silken black panties.

Cath looked elegant and in control. Despite her diminutive frame, she completely dominated the room. She was tight with small but deliciously firm tits. Her dark hair streamed down her shoulders, brushing her dark red nipples. She looked comfortable and unashamed standing there in just her black panties. She reached down to where she had set her pants and took the buckle of a small leather belt into her hand.

Heather swallowed, instinctively knowing what that belt was going to be used for.

Cath took the thin, stylish leather belt that once wrapped around her fit waist and pulled it free. She took it in both hands and snapped it in the air, making a sharp sound as she smiled with devious excitement at the little, feminized French maid. "I'm going to beat your little faggot ass, Slave," she teased. "What do you think of that?"

Heather's flesh flushed with excitement. He knew that deep down, he deserved to be hurt by the angry little lesbian.

"I'm going to beat you till you cry and then I'm going to beat you some more. I hate men. You're not a man anymore, but you used to be. That's close enough for me." She snapped the belt through the air, whipping it across Heather's slim thighs, just above the hem of his nylons. His pale flesh showed an instant slash of red and Heather cringed, his eyes wet.

Heather breathed in with the shock of the pain, but he felt himself relax. This was what he was created for. This was his purpose. His body tingled knowing his pain was going to give this harsh, cruel woman some pleasure.

"Turn around and bend over," Cath said. "Show me that pretty little ass of yours."

Heather turned around. He towered over the little brunette but somehow, he couldn't even imagine resisting her stern commands. He knelt forward, his tits pressing against the footboard as he bent low. He pulled up his skirt, folding it over his waist so Cath could see his slim, curved ass.

Cath licked her lips, the soft feminine ass of the tall, slender sissy thrilling her. "Pull your panties down a little," she said. "But keep your thighs together nice and tight. I don't want to see your filthy little penis until I must. Understand?"

"Yes, Ma'am," Heather said as the reached back and peeled his pretty pink panties down his pale thighs.

Cath sighed, her body stirring at the sight, then she pulled back her hand and brought the belt whistling through the air and smacking into Heather's small, round ass. Heather whimpered.

"I want you to understand," Cath said firmly. "You are going to fuck my pretty wife tonight, but it's not for you. None of this is for your pleasure. That is not your dick anymore. It is our dildo. Your pleasure is meaningless. Your body is worthless. You are just a toy." She whipped her belt across Heather's freckled ass again, causing another bright red slash.

Heather understood that none of this was for his pleasure, but he couldn't stop himself from feeling intense pleasure all the same. Every slash of the belt made him feel more comfortable and at ease. Every painful sting of leather against flesh made his dick swell and throb beneath him.

The belt sang through the air and contacted his flesh once more, making him whimper and bite his luscious red lip.

Tori came back into the bedroom wearing a delicate white-lace Teddy. "Oh," she purred. "The poor little thing. You're hurting her."

"It, Darling," Cath corrected. "I'm hurting it. And it's okay. It just needs to understand it's place."

"I'm sure your right," Tori said. "I didn't mean to question you, Sweetie."

"Sissy," Cath said. "Go kiss my wife and show her how eager you are to please her."

Heather straightened up and adjusted his skirt. He curtsied to Cath then walked up to the cute blonde. The woman was so much shorter than Heather that he had to bend at the waist again to bring their lips together. He pushed his mouth to hers and kissed her eagerly.

Tori moaned, her feather soft lips opening for him. Heather pressed his wet tongue into her small mouth and began to caress and explore. As they kissed, Cath whipped him once more across the ass.

"Go stand in the corner," Cath commanded as she walked up and took his place, kissing her pretty blonde wife. They kissed passionately, hands exploring each other's soft bodies. Tori backed up to the bed, sitting on its edge and Cath eagerly kissed her way down the blonde's luscious, curing body. She pulled down on the front of Tori's teddy, pulling the fabric down and exposing her beautiful, natural breasts. She cupped them in her hands and began to kiss and suckle them one by one.

Tori moaned with pleasure, peeking at Heather who stood obediently in the corner, his big dick pressing against his panties and making a bulge against the top of his little flared skirt. Cath had lost all interest in him, focusing all her attention on her bride. She kissed lower down Tori's body, finally bringing her face between the lovely girl's shapely thighs. Tori moaned as she spread her legs wide for her severe, dark haired lover.

Cath pushed her lips to the fabric that covered Tori's wet pussy and gave her sweet little kisses, as her fingers traced down the edges of the fabric. Finding the little snaps at the bottom of her lover's sexy white teddy, she unclasped them with her fingers and exposed her wet slit and little blonde bush. Cath pressed her lips to Tori's cunt and began to caress her pink flesh with an eager wet tongue.

Tori whimpered with pleasure, still looking at the tall, gorgeous redhead who stood in the corner. Cath's fingers parted Tori's glistening pussy lips and she pushed her tongue deep inside the cute blonde's wet cunt. She drank eagerly, slurping Tori's juices and swallowing them down. She pressed her lips to the bead of the lovely blonde's clit and began to suckle it, causing Tori to respond with whimpers and heavy breathing. Tori fell back on the bed, her hands in Cath's dark hair, her eyes closed. Her lips were parted, sounds of pleasure pouring out from between them. Tori arched her back as her whimpers became more frantic, she began to gyrate, her breasts jiggling and her hands clenching. "Yes," she purred. "Oh yes. My love. That's it. That's it." She came with a deep sigh and then giggled with joy as Cath looked up at her, face wet with pussy-juice.

Tori sat up eagerly, took Cath's cheeks in her hands band began to lick her face clean like a mother kitten. "I love you," Tori whispered.

"I love you too," Cath purred back. "Are you ready?"

Tori nodded. Cath turned back towards Heather and commanded, "Get over here Slave. My wife is ready to play with her new dildo."

Heather stepped forward. Tori looked at the tall, elegant sissy, eyes glistening with desire.

"You can take off your panties now," Cath said. "But the rest of your outfit is too cute. Leave it on."

"Yes Ma'am," Heather said. He reached under the little flared skirt and pulled down his delicate lace panties, pulling his large heels through the small leg holes then tossing the underwear aside.

Tori licked her lips, looking at Heather's hard cock pushing out from under his skirt, the swollen purple head exposed. Heather looked at the cute blonde, her teddy pulled down to expose her big, natural tits, and her cunt exposed and glistening with spit and pussy juice. Heather moved between her legs. Tori laid back, her tits rising and falling with her deep excited breaths. Heather came down on top of her, crawling onto the bed. He kissed her lips, his hard cock throbbing against her wet slit as their bodies pressed together.

Heather took his throbbing cock in his soft hand and pushed it to the opening of Tori's pussy, letting it linger there, savoring the heat of her body.

"Fuck me," Tori purred in his ear. "Sweet, beautiful boy... fuck me."

Behind him, he could hear Cath's voice growl, "You heard her, get to work."

He heard the familiar whistle of the leather belt cutting through the air and recognized the burn as it slashed across the tender flesh of his soft, pale ass. He whimpered softly and pushed his cock inside the soft opening of the cute little blonde.

Tori sighed with deep pleasure, no longer concerning herself with his pain. "Yes," she purred. "I can feel her blood, pulsing through her big, beautiful cock."

The belt slashed across Heather's ass again. Tori moaned with pleasure as Heather's body shuddered inside her. Heather rocked his hips, feeling the soft warmth of Tori's velvety pussy. He began gently fucking her to the music of her soft, whimpering voice. Every time he pressed forward, gently thrusting into the little blonde, Cath whipped the belt across his tender ass. Thrust-slash; thrust-slash; Tori purring with ecstasy, Cath breathing hard with the exertion of her rage as she slapped Heather's pale curved ass over and over. Heather's ass burned like fire as his cock tingled with a thrilling sensation of engulfing wetness and yielding flesh. He whimpered, his whole body radiating with energy. Thrust-slash; thrust-slash; Cath continued to punish him for every moment of pleasure, but the sharp sting of the leather belt was pleasure for him too and he whimpered with pleasure, fucking the cute little blonde harder.

"Yes," Tori whimpered. "Oh yes. You're such a wonderful, pretty little-man. You are beautiful toy."

Heather felt his penis throbbing with electricity as he pushed back and forth through Tori's compliant pussy. She wrapped her legs around his slender hips and hooked the back of his skinny legs with her heels, panting with pleasure and rolling her body against him. Heather could hear the belt sing through the air, over and over as he moved his dick deep inside Tori's blissfully wet snatch.

Tori's whole body shuddered and her high voice raised higher. She smiled as the orgasm moved through her, gentle but profound, filling her with ecstasy. When it passed, she clung to him, her legs and arms tight against him, holding him deep inside her. She kissed his cheek and whispered, "Sweet, sweet boy. You made me cum so nice." She raised her voice and told Cath, "You have to try her. She has the most beautiful dick. You will love it."

"You know I have no interest in filthy boys," Cath said.

"Please, do it for me. I know you will love it. You said yourself, she's just a toy, just a dildo with a pulse."

Cath smiled her consent, thrilled to hear her own words echoed back to her.

Tori rolled, moving Heather onto his back. His ass burned as it brushed against the silk sheets. Cath had whipped his pretty little ass to a dark red bruise. Tori kissed him, then she sat up, spun around and lowered her still wet pussy to his gorgeous face. Heather instantly went to work, kissing and sucking Tori's pussy as she braced her hands against his ribcage and began to grind against him mouth.

Cath stripped out of her panties and moved up, straddling Heather's soft, feminine body. She hovered over his throbbing erection. Cath leaned forward and the two lesbians kissed. Tori reached down and took Heather's fat erection in her hand, pointing it to Cath's slit. The slim, dark haired girl slowly lowered herself down. She purred with pleasure as Heather's throbbing meat filled her tight cunt. The two girls kissed passionately as they rode his face and cock, gently caressing each other's soft skin.

Heather really did feel like a toy now, as the two girls rode him, his little skirt pushed up to expose his cock, Tori's cunt grinding against his obedient mouth. He could hear the wet sounds of their passionate kissing as they ignored him completely; just a toy; just a body to use.

They rocked their bodies faster and faster, fucking his face and cock with eager gyrating hips. Their tongues darted frantically in and out of each other's wet mouths. He felt his body radiating with intensity as an orgasm began to form deep inside him. He felt himself moving closer and closer to that ecstatic release until he was about to climax. Suddenly a thought entered his mind. This wasn't for his pleasure. He was just a toy.

His orgasm suddenly vanished, he groaned with frustration into the wet cunt that pressed down on his mouth as another wet cunt rocked against his still raging hard-on. He felt distant from his body; as numb as if he really was made of plastic while the two lesbians continued to get each other off on his little doll body. Soon the pair of lesbians shuddered and moaned, kissing each other's mouths, necks and breasts. He could feel the orgasm moving through the two bodies above him and he envied their release. Their hot bodies ground down on him as their voices whimpered and moaned. He could hear the course of their climax in those intense, pleasure-filled voices, but their seductive passion could not touch him. He was a dildo and a pretty mouth for them to use. His own orgasm would not return.

The two girls collapsed onto the bed, holding each other and sighing with contentment. Heather sat up and stared at his hard, unfulfilled cock, still standing up from his lap, pushing its way past his skirt.

"Were done playing with our toy, so you can put it away now," Cath said.

Heather pushed his skirt down over his erection and stood up, looking for his panties.

"We still have you for the night," Cath pointed out. "Fix yourself up and start cleaning this place. Perhaps I'll let you bathe us later if you promise not to touch your filthy boy parts."

Heather thought about gently bathing the two girls, pressing a warm, soapy sponge across their soft, supple skin and then lovingly patting them dry, but it did nothing to ease the throbbing erection he was trying to conceal with his skirt. "I promise," he said.

Interrogated by a Cruel Tranny

Harris pulled at his restraints. He was very secure. There was no way for him to get loose. His wrists were held by steel shackles, arms outstretched, spread by taut steel chains that connected to the walls of the dank garage. His legs spread, limp dick dangling, ankles shackled to the floor. He felt powerless and terrified, which was exactly what he was paying for. The chains were secure, the location secluded, and his interrogator would not only be playing a role, but actually believe herself to be a CIA interrogation expert. The only way Harris could get free was if he chickened out and used the safe-word he'd been given.

Once he said the safe word, the fantasy would end.

He had asked Tanya Payne (the Amazonian vixen who ran the dollhouse) if he could just say the safe-word and take a break, or have the intensity dialed down but Tanya had told him no. She said there had to be consequences, otherwise this was would just be like play acting with a cheap hooker. He could use his safe-word any time he wanted, but his payment was non-refundable. He went all the way, or he went home a failure.

Harris felt a tinge of terrified excitement when the tall red-head walked into the room. He had heard that Tanya Payne used transgender slaves to fulfil her client's fantasies, but this could not be one of them. The slender redhead had a willowing frame and soft, porcelain white skin. She almost had the same breathtaking presence as the beautiful Tanya Payne herself. She had firm, breasts that looked natural and slightly small on her six-foot frame. She wore a tight blouse, black pumps, nylons, and a black cotton skirt that made her look like a lawyer or an accountant from a softcore porn.

Her heels clicked on the raw, concrete floor as she walked in front of him, looking through a file she held in her graceful hands, ignoring him completely. "Harris Mongomery Wallace," she finally said in a cold, condemning voice. "My name is Heather, and I'm the only friend you have in this dungeon, and your only chance to ever walk out of it. I need you to tell me the names of all your co-conspirators. I need you to give me a list of safe houses and contacts. And finally I need you to tell me all the details of your plan. If you do all these things I'm prepared to reward you. If you do not, I'm going to have to punish you."

"I'm innocent," he pleaded.

She turned sharply, her gorgeous features alive with anger, red hair flaring as she spun, whipping across his skin, her pale skin had a deep red hue. "Lying to me is not a good start," she said as she raised her hand high, then brought it down, slapping him across the face.

Harris gasped at the force of the blow. His face stung and he felt a little light headed, but his cock tingled with excitement. "I'm not telling you shit," he said.

Again, she slapped her silky-smooth hand across his coarse, whiskered face. The force surprised him again and his face felt hot and red.

She was taller than him without her heels, but with her heels she was so tall she had to bend her gorgeous, slender body in able to bring her face directly in front of his. "I'm going to hurt you, Sweetie," she said. "You do understand that, right?"

His body shuddered with expectation.

She leaned in and softly kissed his cheek. He could smell her perfume and the clean, fresh sent of her soft red hair. She straightened up and turned. As she strolled towards a small steel table across from him, he watched her small, perfectly curved ass as it swayed in her tight black skirt.

She stood at the table, her hand hovering over it as if carefully choosing his fate. Finally, she took a black riding crop into her hand. She walked slow and elegant back to him. She took the crop and touched his chin with it, then lightly traced the leather tip down his throat. She seemed to study his bound body like it was a mildly interesting medical experiment. She traced her crop across the flesh of his chest, the leather pressing against his nipples one by one, making them harden to tight points. The black leather tip traced down his belly, his pelvic bone, then circled to his hip as she began to circle him.

He felt the leather touch his bare ass then pull away. He heard the leather whistle as it cut through the air and came down with a stinging slash on his trembling buttocks. He whimpered as the pain hit then passed, leaving him with just a pulsating line of energy across his ass.

"Names," the gorgeous redhead demanded before whipping him once more.

Two bright red lines were painted across the pale flesh of his ass.

"Locations," she ordered as she slashed him again.

His ass tingled like a shallow cut and he breathed in with a hiss.

"Contacts," she said with another sharp movement of her arm, bringing the crop across his bare flesh once more.

Four intersecting red lines decorated his butt. He breathed deeply, feeling them pulsate and burn.

She circled around in front of him once more. She ignored his hard-on as she traced the tip of her weapon up his thigh. Bringing the crop to his hairy balls she teased him momentarily, tickling his sensitive flesh. Then came the strike. It was just a little tap; just a flick of the wrist that brought the crop down and up again sharply, smacking against his balls, but it made him howl with pain.

She laughed and pressed her luscious lips to his ear. Her red hair tickled his face and neck as she purred. "I'm supposed to make you talk as quick as possible, but I hope you hold out a long time. I love hurting men like you."

His cock throbbed with excitement even as his balls throbbed with pain. She looked down at his cock as she traced the tip of her crop over it. She followed the line of a protruding vein up to his swollen purple tip. His erection was standing straight and proud, but when she smacked his bulbous cock-head it shrunk instantly to limpness.

He whimpered in agonized shudders as she laughed with delight. She walked away from him, swaying gracefully as she went back to the table. She selected another tool, this one a long black whip.

He breathed in hard and held his breath, wincing as she slashed her whip through the air with a crack. It cut through the air, stopping just short of his face. She laughed at his terrified expression and stepped forward. She worked the whip once more, this time making contact, tracing a snake of raw red flesh across his chest.

Harris whimpered, the pain sharp and almost overwhelming, chasing away every other sensation from his mind. He felt an overwhelming awareness of the moment, his eyes wet with tears, the dank air of the darkened make-shift dungeon, the sound of leather as the redhead coiled the whip back, preparing to strike him once more.

He bit his lip, his whole-body clenching in expectation of the coming blow. When it came, he still wasn't prepared. The leather cut across his belly like a line of fire moving across his soft, pale skin. He howled and she stood, watching him with an intense look in her beautiful eyes. Harris looked in those eyes, her gorgeous presence making the bite of pain feel more sensual.

"Still nothing to say?" she asked.

He couldn't make himself speak, but he shook his head slightly. Her eyes seemed to light up with happiness. She dropped the whip onto the floor and strolled up to him like a model moving down a catwalk. As she moved into his space he could feel and smell her.

"I'm glad you're not talking," she whispered, "because I really want to punish you."

Harris wondered what punishments could still be in store for him and if he would be able to endure them.

Heather moved away from him again and stopped an arm's reach away. "I guess I'm going to have to punish you now," she said loudly, as if to a room of silent observers. He glanced at a camera on the wall and wondered how many people might be watching his humiliation take place.

The thought was interrupted as Heather began to slide her hands up her gorgeous long legs. He stared as she reached under her skirt and began to peel a pair of pink, lace panties down her gorgeous, slender thighs. She slid them down her incredibly long, nylon covered legs until they reached her sexy heels then she carefully stepped out of them, bending in front of him like a majestic, red-haired goddess. She picked up her underwear, wadding it into her fist. She straightened up and moved towards him. She tugged on his chin, forcing his mouth open so she could shove the pretty, pink panties between his lips, gagging him. His dick was tingling as she forced the pink lace into his wet mouth. He realized for a moment that he couldn't speak. How was he supposed to say the safe word?

It didn't matter. He had no intention of using the safe-word anyway.

The amazing redhead began to open her blouse. Harris wondered how this was considered punishment instead of reward as she revealed her slim, tight torso and firm, perky breasts. She threw her blouse aside and began to unzip her skirt. He scanned down her flowing frame, tapered chest, delicate ribcage, tiny flat belly and incredibly slender waist flaring out to full, smooth hips. The skirt pulled down some more; soft feminine skin sprinkled with tiny freckles. She pulled the skirt down more and suddenly he saw her huge, cock, dangling between her taut, silken legs.

She let the skirt fall to the floor and stood there in just her heels and nylon stockings. She took her big dick in her soft, beautiful hand and stroked it, making it hard almost instantly. He stared at it with terror. He tried to speak but the panties muffled his voice. She reached forward and took his own cock in her hand. She laughed. "You're supposed to be the man, but I'm much bigger than you, aren't I?"

She giggled as she slapped his limp cock with her hard-on and he fought back the strange arousal he was feeling. Her hand felt incredible on his sensitive flesh as she whacked her cock against his slowly growing dick, making a loud slap. One hand on her cock, one hand on his, she stroked them both with a gentle rhythm. He couldn't fight it. He was hard in her grasp after just a few moments.

She laughed at his hard-on. "Better, but you still don't measure up, do you, Sweetie?" It was true, her dick was fatter and longer than his by nearly half, and as she slapped her hard-on against his, he could tell it was stronger as well. "Are you ready for your punishment, Little Bitch?"

He shook his head but it didn't matter, only the safe-word could stop the fantasy from playing out and somehow this Amazonian tranny was doing whatever she wanted.

She circled around behind him. She reached down and spread his ass-cheeks as she lowered her body. He felt the fat head of her big, tranny cock pressing against his tight, virgin asshole. His body trembled with the realization that his fantasy had gotten out of control. But somehow, the idea of giving up control, not just pretending, but truly surrendering it, filled him with a strange tingling rush. The panties that gagged him also gave him the strength to surrender something he would never dare surrendering on his own.

There was something profound and transcendental about giving in to something he did not desire. Not that it mattered what he thought. It was clear the gorgeous shemale was going to do whatever she wanted, and continue doing it until she heard him utter that now useless safe-word.

His body clenched as the fat dick began to penetrate him. His sphincter tightened, trying to fight off the invasion of hot, throbbing meat, but the tranny pushed through his body's unconscious resistance, pressing into the soft warm flesh inside him. Harris felt a powerful aching pain rack through his colon as the gorgeous redhead's big cock split him open.

She leaned close to him, her soft tits pressing against his back. "Tell me what I need to know, Little Bitch," she purred into his ear, but of course he couldn't tell her anything. He simply whimpered into the wet ball of lace that clogged his mouth. Her soft, smooth hands traced down his side as she stood motionless, her cock buried deep in his rectum. She tickled his skin with her fingertips, causing goosebumps even as the fat rod inside him throbbed and radiated heat through his insides. Her fingertips found the fresh wound her whip had made on his belly and she traced it, making him whimper again.

"Very well," she finally said. "Let the punishment begin."

She took hold of his hips and held his body steady as she drew her massive cock backwards. He could feel every ridge and every vein of her impressive meat as it rubbed through the soft flesh of his tender opening. She pulled herself almost completely out. He could feel his rectum tight against the soft, swollen tip of her cock as it hovered just inside his hole.

His body trembled with terrible expectation as she held herself just inside him. He could feel her pulse in the mushroom head of her cock as it throbbed. Finally, her grip grew even tighter on his hips and her dick plunged deep inside him.

He groaned into a mouthful of panties as pain seared through the depths of him.

"You belong to me now, Bitch," Heather said as she drew her cock back and slammed it forward again. "My little faggot bitch."

He groaned and cried and shook with pain as she savagely pounded his ass. The pain was intense but deep down he knew: he wouldn't use that safe-word now even if he could. On some deep and powerful level, he really did belong to Heather. She had claimed some deep, dark weakness inside him and it was worth the pain of her brutal cock to feel that ownership taking hold of him.

His asshole was raw and inflamed, the depths of his rectum spasming as Heather's huge prick slammed back and forth inside him. His limp dick flopped between his legs with every thrust and his swaying body felt like it was dangling from the chains that bound him to the wall. The sound of the Tranny's hips slapping against his ass was punctuated by the muffled sound of his cries. He pictured the gorgeous redhead behind him, beautiful face, slender body, gorgeous tits and long legs, standing in her heels and nylons as she pounded his helpless, chained body, and it made his dick tingle and stir.

Even as the pain of her dick impaling him, driving him back and forth against his shackles thundered through him, his dick began to swell and harden. Again and again, the breathtaking tranny pummeled his tender insides with her iron-hard prick and again and again he shuddered, whimpered and felt a thrill of finally being a true and complete slave.

He could feel her pulsating in his abused asshole, her pulse increasing and her heat magnifying as she became more and more excited. Harder and harder he was jerked back and forth, the shackles cutting into his wrists and ankles. She began to moan with pleasure as she hammered him, fucking him like a marionette dangling on a set of strings. His whipped butt-cheeks burned with every thrust of her hips, driving her flesh against his with a harsh slap.

"Yes," Heather cried out. "Who's the whore now? Who's the whore now, little bitch?"

Harris felt the hot sprays of semen shooting deep into his rectal cavern, filling him up with sticky jizz. Wave after wave of cum shot inside him as Heather shivered with orgasm behind him. Finally, she relaxed. She leaned her long slender body against his, pressing her hard, pink nipples to his back as she hugged him and kissed the top of his head. She pulled her cock from inside him and stepped away.

She circled in front of him, once again the image of graceful, feminine perfection. She put her thumb on his jaw and yanked it open so she could pull her wet panties from his mouth.

He gasped. His ass ached and throbbed and his muscles all burned with pain.

She seemed oblivious to him as she took the underwear that had been shoved in his mouth and slid them back on, daintily tucking her big, limp cock.

She looked up at him and smiled wickedly. "Are you ready to tell me what I want to hear, or should I punish you again? I can go all night Sweetie."

He began to give her the information. He listed off imaginary names, made up safe houses and non-existent contacts.

"Good boy," she said, petting his hair as he listed the information, her gorgeous feminine body pressing against him. He couldn't stop himself from staring at her beautiful face and cute tits. He was still erect, and that erection swelled even more as he felt her slender body brushing against him.

"Very good boy," she said. "Like I said, you give me what I want and you get a reward." Suddenly she dropped to her knees in front of him. She looked up at him, her beautiful face framed in fiery red as she took his cock in her hand and guided it toward her luscious young lips.

He moaned with pleasure as Heather pressed his dick into her wet mouth. His pulse deepened and he moaned with delight. He looked down at the tall, fair-skinned vixen as she slurped his cock down her narrow throat. Her slender body was flawless, her hair bouncing has her head bobbed along his shaft. Harris breathed heavy, the angelic vixen's luscious lips tracing wet trails along the bulging meat of his throbbing cock.

"Oh yes," he cried as Heather's fingertips caressed his thighs and her mouth caressed his prick. "Oh yes, I'm going to cum."

Her gorgeous eyes looked up at him as if welcoming his seed as she continued to suck him in a steady, consistent rhythm.

His toes curled and his fists clenched. His arms and legs tightened against the chains that held him in his uncomfortable position, but all he could feel was his ecstasy building. His balls tightened and quivered and his dick began to twitch, finally shooting a wad of cream into the lovely young tranny's wet mouth. She continued to suck him, her eager mouth sliding along his shaft, cum running across the soft flesh of her lips and smearing along his pole as he fired spurt after spurt of thick white seed into her little pink mouth.

When he was done draining his balls in her mouth she stood up. She turned and spat his cum onto the floor in front of his feet and told him, "Thank you for your cooperation. The guards will be back shortly to take you back to holding to await trial for your crimes."

She slid on her skirt, slipped into her blouse, and strolled out the door.

From her private office, where she watched the whole encounter on camera, Tanya was a little surprised. It did seem like her newest doll, who was normally very obedient, had gone slightly off script. She supposed it was due to Tanya's suggestions, making Heather into an eager interrogator who loved to push the line. Tanya had actually enjoyed it quite a lot. she loved seeing her client's limits tested and expanded and she loved watching men broken and seeing their precious anal virginities robbed. It had worked out for the best. She was glad Heather had gone further than expected. Harris looked absolutely delighted with his fantasy as the nurses came and unchained him from the wall. The whole scene had turned Tanya on so much that now she felt the urge to find a nervous and sniveling young man so that she could peg him ruthlessly.

Tanya picked up her phone and called her assistant. "Bridgette, ready the limo, I'm going to take a drive down to the village this evening."

His Pretty Asian Anniversary Present

"You still haven't explained to me what this place is?" Tod said to his pretty wife of three years.

The short, well-built brunette smiled in that taunting way she had. "If I did that," she said. "Where would be the surprise?"

Tod smiled back at his cute little full-figured wife. She had flown him out to some island he'd never heard of for a surprise anniversary present. Now they sat in a beautiful penthouse suite waiting for the gift to be delivered. "Shouldn't we get dressed?" Tod asked, fishing for clues. "Don't you want to go get some food later?"

Crystal smiled cryptically, wearing nothing but a little black silk slip, her hair done, full makeup on. She looked absolutely flawless and deliciously devious, hiding her little secret from him. "We'll order room service later," she said.

He wore nothing but silk boxers and he kept catching his cute young wife peeking at his fit, lean body, but she had refused to fool around. Soon the doorbell rang and Crystal hoped excitedly to her feet and hurried to the door. He stood as well and walked behind her.

When Crystal pulled open the door he saw the sexiest young Asian woman he'd ever seen in his life standing on the other side. The tall, caramel-skinned girl was all was stunningly slender with startlingly luscious curves. She wore nothing but black lace underwear and a transparent lace robe. He was amazed the girl could be walking the hallways of the resort hotel like that.

Tod waited with expectation and a tinge of excitement for his jealous wife to lose her mind and start berating the lost little Asian slut with vicious insults but instead she smiled as she looked at her, studying her flawless, full curves.

The slim, caramel skinned girl stood in the hallway. She seemed shy, and her gaze dropped under the gaze of Crystal's appraising eye. It was almost impossible for Tod to imagine a woman that gorgeous being insecure. She clearly had cosmetic surgery done, no natural woman could look that flawless.

"What's your name," Crystal demanded.

"Ting," the girl practically squeaked.

"And what are you?" Crystal asked.

"I'm your husband's anniversary present," she said.

"Get in here," Crystal said to a slender little Asian. "We've been waiting. Move." She gave the thinner girl a rough shove on her delicate brown flesh, sending her hurrying into the room, her eyes on the floor.

Tod felt a rush of excitement, not just from seeing the gorgeous girl, but from his wife's rough treatment of her. He had always got a secret rush from what a bitch his wife could be to other women, especially pretty ones. She had a vicious jealous streak that always seemed inexplicably hot to him. Waitresses, friend's wives, random young girls walking by the house, none of them escaped Crystal's scorn or hateful gaze.

She turned to him now and smiled sweetly. "Remember how you always wanted to have a three-way?" she said.

"Well yeah," he said. "But I thought you said you would never be able to see me with another woman?"

"That's the best part," Crystal said. "This isn't a woman."

Tod looked at the gorgeous Asian. "What are you talking about?"

"Show him," Crystal growled at the shy little doll.

Ting took hold of her little black panties and rolled them her slim thighs, revealing a tiny dick and hairless balls.

They both laughed. "What the hell is that?" Tod asked.

"They call it her sissy clit," Crystal said wickedly. "Poor thing was born with that little thing."

"Those tits though," Tod said. "I guess she wasn't born with those."

Crystal smiled. "Amazing, right? Everything you'd want in a little Asian bimbo minus the one thing I don't want. You can do anything you want to her. Happy anniversary."

"You sure?" he asked, part of him worried it was some kind of test.

"Whore," Crystal said to the petite, nervous Asian without taking her wicked, excited gaze from Tod's face. "Why don't you strip so my husband can see what a generous wife I am."

Tod watched in amazement as the little brown girl stripped, revealing her tight, flawless body and full, flowing curves. She had one hand over her tiny dick and one hand across her massive chest, looking at the floor like a lost little puppy.

"Turn around," Tod said. "Let me see that ass."

The little tranny turned slowly, nervously in front of him. She had an incredible heart shaped ass. He licked his lips, imagining how it would feel to touch that soft, silky brown skin. Tod looked from it to his excited wife. "Why's she so shy?" he asked.

Crystal giggled. "That's the best part. This little bimbo is a brainwashed slave. I ordered her personality down to every last detail and she doesn't even know it. She probably has fake little memories dancing through her empty skull telling her to be shy, submissive and desperately, almost pathetically horny."

Tod looked at the breathtaking creature again. "Honey," he said to his beautiful young wife. "Why don't you give her a little spank."

Crystal smiled and brought her hand down in a sharp arc, slapping Ting's ass hard. Ting jumped slightly with the force of impact and let out a feminine little squeak, but her big, firm ass only jiggled slightly. Crystal gave him a naughty look then slapped Ting's ass harder, causing the tranny to cry out.

"How's that feel, Little Whore?" Crystal asked.

"Good," the little whore whimpered.

"Why's it feel good?" Crystal asked, her voice full of excitement.

"Because I'm a stupid sissy slut," Ting answered.

Crystal cackled with laughter. "Isn't she just perfect?"

"You're perfect," Tod said as he stepped up, took his wife into his arms and kissed her passionately. The two held each other close, the heat of their bodies stirring each other's excitement even more. Crystal stayed in his arms and turned to look at the gorgeous young tranny, still standing there with her ass exposed.

"Make her turn around," Tod said.

"Turn around whore," Crystal said with vicious glee.

Ting turned back to face him and he saw that she had a tiny erection pointing back up at her beautiful face. The couple laughed in unison. Crystal whispered into his ear, "You got the little slut all worked up."

"Why don't you play with her little dick a bit?" Tod asked his wife.

Crystal smiled shyly back at him. "Are you sure? She's your present."

"I can't imagine a better present. Don't worry. I won't get jealous. It's not like a real dick. It's just a little toy. Go ahead. Give it a tug, give it a kiss, do whatever you like."

Crystal strolled up to the exotic little doll and asked her in a delicious purr, "Do you want me to play with that little hard-on of yours?"

Ting nodded eagerly and Crystal slapped her face. "No one cares what you want, Slave."

The breathtaking Asian bimbo breathed deep as if the slap was what she wanted more than anything. Her whole body seemed to shiver with unconscious delight, her huge tits raising with her deepening breath.

Crystal dropped to her knees and looked back at Tod as she reached forward and caressed the Tgirl's slender brown rod. She leaned closer, parted her lips and let the small dick slip into her wet mouth.

Tod watched in amazement as his beautiful wife sucked the shemale's small but rigid dick. She watched him out of the corner of her eyes as her full lips enveloped the little pink prick. The tranny was moaning with pleasure, her head thrown back, shimmering black hair cascading down. The sound of Ting's soft, feminine moaning mixed with the filthy sound of Crystal's mouth slurping on the throbbing pink rod.

Todd peeled off his boxers, unleashing his fat, throbbing erection. He ran his hand across it, watching his beautiful wife on knees. Tod walked up to the woman he loved and pushed his throbbing cock into her face.

She let the Tranny's dick slip from her mouth and wrapped her lips around Tod's fat cock. Her mouth was enticingly wet and he could feel her saliva running down his fat, throbbing shaft. She slid him out of her mouth and smiled at him. She stroked both cocks beside each other and said, "Look at her little dick baby. You think she ever walked around believing she was a man?"

"I hope not," Tod said. "That would be tragic."

Crystal giggled and took Tod's fat cock back into her wet mouth. Her pretty face was distorted by her mouth stretching around the girth of his pulsating manhood, but she worked her lips up and down his pole, gazing up at him lovingly. He caressed her soft, brown hair watching her work his meat into her throat. She stroked him with her narrow throat then washed him in saliva and pulled him back out from between her lips, glistening and dripping with spit.

"You're all lubed up now Honey," she purred. "Go fuck her. Go fuck that little whore's ass while I play with her sad, sissy clit."

Tod moved around behind the petite Asian doll. He kicked her feet wider apart to expose her ass. On the other side of the tranny's little brown body, Crystal pulled her slip up over her head, revealing her own magnificent curves. Tod noted his wife's freshly shaved cunt and he longed to kiss her there. Crystal put her hands on her soft knees and leaned forward once more, wrapping her lips around Ting's dick.

Tod stood behind Ting, holding his spit drenched cock in his hand. "Spread your cheeks little whore," he told her. Ting leaned slightly forward as she reached back and spread her perfectly curved ass-cheeks with her graceful little hands. Tod moved closer and began to push his fat cock into Ting's tight sissy-cunt.

Ting may have been shy, but she took his fat cock like a seasoned professional. The tranny's asshole seemed to grip his throbbing manhood, pulsating with pressure as she flexed her sphincter, massaging his prick.

"She's so tight," Tod moaned.

Crystal took the tranny's prick between two fingers, stroking it as she looked up at her pretty, Asian face. "How does my husband's cock feel in your tight little sissy cunt, whore?"

"Good," Ting whimpered, her voice high and strained as Tod penetrated deep inside her slender body.

"And how does my mouth feel on your pathetic little sissy clit?" Crystal had a vicious look in her beautiful eyes as she stared up that the slender Asian doll.

"Good," Ting whimpered.

Tod's cock pressed deeper, burying to the base in the Tgirl's soft ass.

Crystal continued staring into the tranny's dark eyes as she asked, "Do you ever wish you had a real cock, so you wouldn't have to get fucked in the ass by strangers?"

Crystal lit up with excitement when she saw the look on Ting's face, obviously finding a nerve buried deep inside the little tranny's brainwashed mind. Crystal laughed with joy, stroking harder. "You do!" she roared. "You wish you could be a real man instead of a little piece of fuck-meat for guys like my husband to use... Sweetie, fuck her harder. She needs to be reminded what she is." With that Crystal took Ting's hard little prick back between her luscious red lips.

Tod began to rock his hips, humping the hot little Asian ladyboy harder.

There was a mirror across the far wall and on it he could see the entire scene. The Asian shemale was slightly bent, one hand on one of her luscious tits, her other in his wife's soft hair. He could see his own fat rod moving between their bodies as it penetrated deep into the tranny's tight asshole. Each thrust of his hips pushed Ting's cock deep into his wife's sweet mouth, causing his wife to make a wet slurping sound. He could see his wife's eyes turned upwards, watching the tranny's gorgeous tits as they jiggled above her.

Ting's soft, feminine whimpering filled the room with lush intensity.

Tod wrapped an arm around Ting's tiny waist as his other hand traced up the shemale's petite body. He felt her taught, caramel skin, her pillow soft tit, her long slender neck. He brought his hand up to her face and she immediately began to suck on one of his fingers. He savored the delicious feeling of wet suction on his finger as he pounded the Tgirl's tight round ass.

Crystal stood up suddenly and took a handful of the tranny's shimmering black hair. She used it like a leash, pulling the girl behind her as she walked towards the bed. Tod's fat cock slipped out of Ting's hole as she was led across the room to the bed. Crystal pressed her lips to the sexy little ladyboy's mouth and they kissed. Tod felt excitement course through him as he watched the two feminine figures hold each other, kissing and caressing.

Crystal moved back onto the bed, laying on her back and spreading her legs. Ting followed Tod's beautiful young bride onto the bed, crawling her way up until her face was between the gorgeous woman's shapely thighs. Ting bowed her head down and began to kiss Crystal's cunt. The tiny, feminized doll was on all fours, ass in the air, head buried in Crystal's delicious pussy. The gorgeous Asian was bowed down in such supplication that she looked like a devotee, worshiping at the altar of feminine beauty and fertility.

Tod stepped up to the edge of the bed and ran one of his hands along the delicate line of the tranny's supple spine, his fat cock resting on the pillow of her ass. He savored the sight for a moment, his wife moaning in pleasure, Ting slurping eagerly between her legs; both bodies enticing and irresistible in the soft hotel-room light. Tod put both hands on Ting's beautiful ass and used his thumbs to spread her cheeks. He moved his hips and pressed his throbbing cock once more into her slender asshole.

The rewarding little purr the tranny made when his fat pole invaded her tight rectum filled Tod with a thrilling sense of heat. He began to pound her tight ass harder.

Crystal moaned as the shemale's mouth worked eagerly at her wet cunt, slurping and licking and smearing her pretty face with slick, flowing juices. Tod held her magnificent curved hips and pumped them as he rammed his cock deep inside her. Ting whimpered with every thrust and Crystal whimpered too, feeling Tod's power vibrate through the tranny's body. He listened to the music of ecstasy in both of those sweet, feminine voices as he rammed Ting's tight ass with an unrelenting rhythm.

The little whore took the fucking like a champ, pressing her soft ass back against him as he thrusted into her. The tranny's hand reached back, grabbing her own little prick as she got ass-fucked with her face buried in hot, wet pussy. The room was full of blissful whimpers, Crystal rubbing her clit as Ting licked her tight pussy, Ting stroking her little cock as Tod fucked her tight asshole. The two feminine voices seemed to feed off each other, rising higher and higher in pitch.

Tod watched both those beautiful bodies begin to tremble and shake as they both began to shudder with orgasm. Crystal locked her thighs against Ting's face, grabbing the Asian's silky black hair as she humped her face, panting. Ting's whole body twitched and rocked as her tiny balls tightened and she shot her sperm onto the bedspread. Tod released his grip of the tranny's hips, letting her drained body collapse down into the mess she had made.

Crystal released the pressure of her legs on the tranny's face and fell back, closing her eyes and staring at the ceiling.

Tod stroked his cock, looking at their sexy, limp bodies.

Ting was the first to stir. She rose to her hands and knees and looked back over her slender brown shoulder at him. Her eyes were still burning with lust. She turned and began to crawl towards him, her big, artificial breasts barely moving beneath her.

Ting moved to the edge of the bed, resting on her slender brown elbows and knees. She smiled up at him as she took his fat dick in her mouth and began to suck it down her throat with expertise. She gazed at him with submission in her dark, exotic eyes, swallowing his massive pole with her tiny mouth.

His wife moved beside her, wrapping her arm around the tranny's slim shoulders as if they were suddenly the best of girlfriends, she watched Ting work. "You're good at that, Little Whore," she said.

Ting turned her obedient gaze from him to his wife. She continued to work his throbbing meat in and out of her throat as she stared as his wife's pretty face. Ting finally let his meat slip from between her lips and smiled demurely at the woman he loved. Crystal kissed Ting sweetly, their mouths hovering just over his fat prick. Their kiss grew more passionate as they caressed each other's hair, Crystal's free hand stroking Tod's cock.

Tod began to wonder who's present this really was as he watched the two beautiful faces, kissing each and teasingly gazing into each other's pretty eyes. Crystal stroked him faster, but her attention was focused on the Asian shemale, their pink tongues dancing in each other's mouths.

Tod's cock began to throb with more and more intensity as he watched the soft, feminine faces alive with lust as they kissed above his cock. Crystal's grip tightened on his shaft, pumping harder as Ting's hand worked down Crystal's chest and cupped her pale breast, squeezing her soft, milk-white flesh.

Tod's balls began to tighten and he moaned with pleasure and excitement. The two pretty faces recognized the sound of ecstasy growing in his voice and they turned towards his pulsating cock-head, mouths open, tongues extended, cheeks pressed together. Tod's dick twitched as his orgasm hit and he fired the first burst of jizz into the soft flesh of those beautiful faces.

Crystal moved his cock in tight little circles as he came, sending spooge flinging across both their faces, into both their mouths and along the soft, silken lines of their lustrous dark hair. After his balls were drained they turned their attention back to each other, kissing each other's cum drenched mouths and licking semen from each other's flawless skin.

When they were both licked and sucked clean, Crystal gave the petite caramel tranny a pat on the head and said, "Good job. Now go away whore, were all done with you."

Ting sat up, bowed, picked up her clothes and hurried out of the room, not even taking the time to dress until she was in the hallway.

Tod smiled at his wife as she sat up, smiling wickedly. "Thank you for my present," he said.

"It's not over yet," she said. "We have all weekend and you get to pick the next little whore."

Pretty Party Favors

Jen wandered through the party carrying a tray of drinks. He was one of several dolls that worked through the crowd at the corporate retreat in slinky little maid costumes. His consisted of a tight black skirt, fishnet stockings, towering heels and a tight white top. He wore a little pink collar that had his name printed on a silver tag in clear black letters. He smiled demurely at the executives as they pulled strong alcoholic drinks from his tray and pinched his tight, feminine ass.

He was walking by a group of older executives, as one of them said to his friend, "Yes, I meet you there, let me get a quick blowjob first." The man turned his attention to Jen. "You, sissy, get over here."

Jen turned to him and hurried forward as the man unzipped his black dress slacks. He pulled out his fat cock, already massive though only semi-erect and he dangled it from his strong, masculine hand. Jen dropped to his slender knees, balancing his drink tray with one hand as the other reached forward and took a grip of the older man's meaty shaft. Jen opened his luscious lips and extended his little pink tongue, pressing it to the tip of the older man's swelling cock. He looked up at the man, blinking his lustrous eyelashes over his pretty blue eyes as he wrapped his red lips around the man's meat.

The grey-haired man grew instantly hard in Jen's soft, wet mouth and Jen felt a flush of pride. He arched his slender back, showing off his cute little ass as he pressed the man's fat meat deeper. Jen slid the throbbing cock down his throat, messaging it with the soft flesh of his tongue as he worked it in and out of his tight esophagus.

The stranger moaned with pleasure as his fat rod stretched the little blonde tranny's throat with its girth. Jen worked his head back and forth, soft lips cradling the contours of the executives bulging shaft. Men walked by, paying no attention to Jen's head bobbing back and forth along the stranger's hard cock as they took drinks from his carefully balanced tray.

Most said nothing as they took their drinks and kept walking, but some of them were kind enough to give Jen a pat on his little blonde head. Jen felt his own small dick tingling in his tight pink panties as he sucked the fat cock hungrily with his little wet mouth. Jen's soft lips worked back and forth along the hot throbbing shaft, submissive eyes staring up at the man as he ate his rod. The man brought his hands to Jen's head and held it steady, pressing his hips forward and burying his cock deep in Jen's throat as his cock began to pulsate and twitch. He held Jen's head firmly, cock planted deep down the sissy's throat, and began to explode with orgasm.

Jen gulped the hot jizz as it shot down his well-trained throat. The man emptied his balls into the tranny's surgically restricted stomach then slid his softening cock out of his soft little mouth. Jen finished swallowing every drop of her salty meal then stood up, straightening his tight little skirt with one hand and balancing his drink-tray with the other. "Thank you, sir," Jen purred.

The man didn't say anything, but took the last drink from Jen's tray before turning and walking away. Jen took his empty tray and started walking back to the kitchen to get more drinks, stopping along the way to give several more blowjobs. Jen felt good. He was in a calm, receptive state. For corporate parties like this, he wasn't programmed to be anything, just his natural, needy little self. He was lifted out of the base, hypnotic state and told only to be himself and do what comes natural.

Some of the dolls at corporate parties even tried to resist the advances of the executives, but perhaps that was part of the appeal. The older business men seemed to appreciate the variety. Jen couldn't imagine even trying to resist the older, more powerful men. He felt joy and honor every time he swallowed a mouthful of their hot, sticky cum.

As Jen walked towards the pantry, wiping the corners of his mouth, he suddenly recognized a familiar face. In the middle of the crowd, bent halfway over a trashcan was an exotic, slender Asian doll. Her little black skirt was pulled up and her panties pushed to the side as a muscular, bald man fucked her tight, tranny ass. He recognized the Thai ladyboy from somewhere beyond memory. She was somehow etched into the fabric of his deepest dreams and he smiled at her. The name on her little pink collar read "Ting." Ting smiled back at him, recognition in her dark eyes, even as the fat cock in her asshole made her wince and moan. Ting wore a little black and white uniform as well.

Jen wasn't sure what the rules where. He knew on some level he wasn't supposed to recognize his beautiful and exotic lover, but he did. He dropped his empty drink-tray to the floor and stepped up to Ting. He leaned over the trashcan and began to passionately kiss her on the mouth. The two sissy's Botox filled lips smashed together as their pink tongues entwined. Their hands explored each other's hormone softened skin as they bent together, pretty face to pretty face.

Jen could feel hands behind him, exploring his slender legs, moving up the taut skin of his tan thighs. His skirt was rising as a middle-aged executive began to peel it up. Jen felt his thong tighten on his small, hairless balls as the man pulled it, moving it clear of his tight brown asshole.

Jen pulled Ting's top down, exposing her fantastic tits. He pinched the beautiful dolls pink nipples, teasing them with his long red fingernails. Ting purred. Jen felt the heat of a fat cock pressing against the silky soft opening of his tight sissy-cunt. He kissed Ting again as the massive pole began to split him open. The two trannies both moaned into each other's wet mouths as they each got impaled by throbbing cocks.

The men behind them pumped their tight asses harder and harder, jerking their rounded hips as they shoved their hot meat inside them. The two sissies' pretty faces bumped together in a steady rhythm, their mouths open wide trying to catch the other's tongue or lips, hands on each other's perfect, artificial breasts. They held their pink tongues extended, letting them crash together as the men thrust them forward. Men's hands groped them as the two trannies groped each other.

Jen savored the feeling of Ting's hard nipples against her fingertips and palms as he accepted the confusing feeling of hot cock violating his tender ass. There was pain as he was stretched open, and he never got used to the sensation of men's bulbous cockheads rooting around inside his soft flesh, but there was pleasure too. The pleasure of being owned. The pleasure of being useful. The pleasure of being a sexy and desirable. There was also the pleasure of a deep, radiating vibration, emanating from his prostate or perhaps someplace deeper, filling him with a feeling that he knew would give him a release more complete than any that could be experienced by a regular man.

That feeling was building in him now, his lips pressed to his lover's luscious mouth, their tongues lapping at each other as both were reamed by powerful men. Jen could hear the man behind him grunting as he pounded harder and faster. He could see the beautiful look in Ting's pleasure filled face as she felt her own sissy-climax building.

The rigid contours of cock moved back and forth in Jen's tight hole, rubbing the nerves in his sensitive flesh. The man's cock was beautiful. He wondered if powerful men like this ever thought about weak, little dicked men like he had once been. He wondered if they ever considered them for long enough to do more than laugh. They were laughing at him now, he knew, laughing at what had been done to him, what he had become. He didn't care. He just wanted to please them. He just wanted to make their gorgeous, fat dicks spray hot, rewarding fountains of nasty semen. He wanted to shower in the physical approval of real men's bodies as they painted him with delicious sperm.

The man behind him pounded him harder and harder. He could hear the sound of the man's hard dick invading his asshole. He could hear the sound of his own feminine whimpers mixing with the sound of Ting's passionate cries.

Finally, the man behind Jen slammed his cock deep into the sissy's rectum and began to explode with orgasm. The man's body shook, hand tightly gripping Jen's tiny waist as he groaned with pleasure. Jen felt his own body vibrate and flare with a deep, anal orgasm as hot jets of sperm splattered against the soft flesh deep inside him. Ting was crying out, "Yes! Yes!" as her own body gave in to the powerful force of his sissy-climax.

Soon the two shemales were leaning over the trash, relaxed and panting, cheeks resting together. The men had moved on to other distractions and left them there, panties pulled aside, skirts up over their waists, assholes leaking cum.

Ting kissed Jen's beautiful makeup covered face. "I think I missed you," she said. "I think I've been looking for you since whenever the last time I saw you was."

"Me too," Jen said. "I love you."

They kissed passionately once more and then Ting took Jen by the hand. "Come on," she said. "Let's sneak outside and talk a while." Jen nodded and they began to wind through the crowd toward a set of glass doors that led out to a balcony. They reached the balcony and stepped outside into the cool night air, but they were not alone.

They saw a radiant redhead splayed out across a table, her pale skin milky-smooth and sprinkled with freckles. She had been stripped of her uniform and besides her pink collar, which showed her name to be "Heather," she wore nothing but her heels and a tight chastity cage that constricted the flesh of her large, limp cock. Her legs were spread wide, her head hanging over the edge of the table, her firm young tits rolling back and forth as the was fucked at both ends. She had a man's hard cock in either hand, stroking them as her ass and throat were brutally pounded. The four men all groped the smooth skin of her gorgeous young body.

Ting and Jen were both struck by the tall slender dolls beauty and they stood holding hands, watching as she got used. Jen felt his dick tingling and beginning to swell. He wondered if he looked as sexy as this gorgeous redhead when he was getting gangbanged by a crowd of rough, anonymous men.

Heather's lips looked lush and moist as they served as pillows for a stranger's massive erection, rolling back and forth in her mouth and sliding into her long, slender throat. Her ass was soft, tight and feminine, small cheeks smashing down as another stranger crashed against her, driving his penis deep into her rectum. The dicks in each of her graceful hands were throbbing against her long, thin fingers.

Jen moaned softly, watching the carnal display. He felt herself getting completely hard, little prick pushing uncomfortably against the elastic of his tight pink panties.

Ting whispered, "You like her." Then she stepped behind Jen and hugged him from behind. "I like her too," she purred as one of her small brown hands floated up to Jen's chest and worked itself under his uniform top, squeezing one of his deliciously full, silicone breasts. Ting's other hand caressed Jen's thigh, tenderly working up underneath his skirt.

Heather's long, lithe body looked angelic as she took a fat cock in her ass, and slurped another one down her throat. The men pounded into her in an alternating rhythm. Heather's sexy black heels rested above the strong shoulders of the man who fucked her ass, her legs long, smooth and slender. In and out the two cocks went, stretching both her holes with their girth while she tugged on the two other cocks, hovering inches from her gorgeous firm titties.

Ting pulled Jen's dick free of his panties, kissing the back of his neck with her luscious lips as she gently stroked him, both of them watching the show. Jen moaned in his high, feminine voice as the hand of his lover squeezed his sissy-clit, jacking him with tender affection.

Heather's body had no trace of fat accept the silicone and Botox that had been injected and implanted into her, all of it moving with tiny little quivers as she was roughly pounded back and forth by two strong pricks. The men fucked her faster and harder and she took it all with apparent eager submission, her hands still working diligently on jerking the two cocks that sat in her elegant hands.

Ting began to stroke Jen faster too, her rhythm beginning to synch with the thrusting hips of them men fucking Heather. Ting's tongue traced up the back of Jen's neck, tracing a wet path from his spine to his ear. She whispered softly, her sultry feminine voice making him shiver. "I love watching you get excited. I love feeling the heat in your cute little dick." Jen could feel Ting's magnificent tits pressing against his back as his own tit tingled from Ting pinching and tweaking his hard, pink nipple.

The men jack-hammered Heather like a piece of meat, pounding her two holes like they belonged to a mindless sex-doll.

Ting squeezed harder on Jen's throbbing meat, purring into his ear as she lapped at it with her tongue.

The two cocks in Heather's hands began to twitch and spurt cum. Wads of thick white cream began to spurt out onto Heather's small, beautiful tits. Her tits glistened with gewy sprays of spunk. The two men seemed to have an endless supply as wave after wave streamed out in thick, salty jets.

Jen whimpered, seeing all that milky semen, his legs began to shake and his dick began to quiver. Ting released his breast and brought her other hand down beneath his skirt, cupping it over his dick and preparing to catch the nearing explosion.

The man fucking Heather's face pulled his dick from between her Botox filled lips. He was already cumming, shooting cum into her mouth, onto her lips and across the skin of her beautiful, make-up covered face. The man fucking her ass also neared orgasm. Pulling his massive cock from her asshole, he began to stroke it violently with his strong hand. A moment later he was spurting hot jizz across her slender thighs, smooth balls and into the rungs of her cramped chastity cage.

Jen's toes curled in his sexy heels as he began to shoot his sissy-sperm into Ting's soft hand.

"MMMM," Ting purred as the hot semen filled her palm. "That feels so nice. That's my good girl. Give me all of it."

Jen's balls tightened in his little pink panties as he drained them into Ting's soft hand, whimpering as he watched Heather get showered in sperm.

Ting stepped beside Jen as she brought her cum covered hand from out of Jen's panties and lapped at the mess with her little pink tongue. She saw the look on Jen's pretty face and turned her palm towards him, offering him a taste which he eagerly accepted. He looked into the dark eyes of the beautiful Asian with his own radiant blues, eyelashes fluttering as he licked his own sperm from the palm of her delicate hand.

When Ting's hand was spotless the two beautiful, young trannies looked at Heather. The men had all left and she lay there, breathing heavy and recovering from her own climax, covered in four different men's hot, filthy loads. Ting took Jen by the hand and they walked up to the gorgeous redhead.

Before Heather had even noticed them approach they began to press their little pink tongues to her milky white flesh and lick up the semen that decorated her flesh. Heather moaned with pleasure as she looked up and watched the two pretty shemales tongue bathing her. Jen licked at the semen on Heather's balls and between the bars of her restrictive chastity cage, and Ting licked Heather's firm tits clean. Their wet mouths worked up and down Heather's slender body until they met at her belly button and began to kiss each other with tender affection.

Heather reached down and caressed both their lustrous heads of beautiful hair. "Thank you," she said.

They looked up at her and smiled as they straightened up to standing, hand in hand like lifelong best friends. Heather got up off the table and they all stood at the edge of the balcony looking out towards the sea.

After a long time of silence Heather finally said, "I want to escape this place."

"I think we tried that once," Ting said. "I can't remember."

"I have a plan," Heather said.

"Yeah, I think we had a plan once too," Ting said. "But we keep losing it. We won't even be the same people next time we meet."

"I've discovered a trick," Heather said. "I remember everything. Not anything from before, but everything since I started using this trick. I hypnotize myself, like Tanya does to us, only I hypnotize myself to remember. When she hypnotizes me, I still become who she wants me to, but some little part of me remains. No matter who I become, I can still feel that part inside me. It's easy to do. I can teach you guys. Then together, maybe we really can escape."

Ting looked at Jen with wild excitement lighting up her beautiful face. "What do you say?" she asked him.

Jen wasn't sure he really wanted to escape. He couldn't remember anything but the dollhouse. He didn't crave anything but the meaty taste of hot, throbbing cock. He looked at Ting, who smiled beautifully and reassuringly back at him. "Where you go, I go," he promised his beautiful Asian lover.

Then, on the balcony in the fresh night air, the taste of cum on all their lips, Heather taught Jen and Ting how to keep a little part of themselves, no matter who they became.

To be continued...

JennaMastersErotica.blogspot.com

Printed in Great Britain
by Amazon

39203763R00067